Tania Glyde is both provocative writer and performer. Her previous novel, *Clever Girl* (Picador), was translated into French and German. She features in the *Disco 2000* (Sceptre) and *Vox 'N' Roll* (Serpent's Tail) anthologies.

JUNK
DNA
TANIA GLYDE

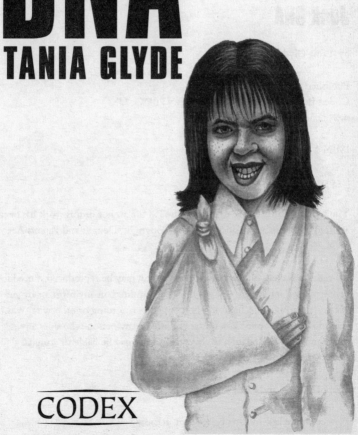

CODEX

Acknowledgements

A big, big thank you to Hayley Ann at Codex for taking on this book (and for being one of the most inspired and original publishers around), to Peter Pavement for a great cover, and to everyone who's kept the faith since I started writing.

Junk DNA

by Tania Glyde

Published in 2000 by
Codex Books, PO Box 148, Hove, BN3 3DQ, UK
www.codexbooks.co.uk

ISBN 1 899598 19 7

Graphic design and typesetting by Slabserif

Printed in the UK by Cox & Wyman, Reading

one

THE PHOTOGRAPH SHOWS THE TOWLE FAMILY around a litter bin on a promenade one summer, Lucy's hair whipping madly at her eyes, her running nose, her cracked lips. Little Lucy aged nine in a red anorak that matches the two dark mists high on her cheeks, her head cricked away from the green and gold bin, which is the same height as she is; and there are Mr and Mrs Towle, the bin rising and forcing the viewer's interest from their crotches, suggestively peekabooed by flapping macs and plastic bags.

This is a typical Towle family snap, this frame which occurred during a brief flurry of movement as Mrs Towle took part of Lucy's upper body and tried to bend it to an approximation of something 'not round-shouldered'.

Lucy has no idea what she is on about. Like the exhortation, "Mark her Lucy!" and the subsequent, "Chrissake!" in PE at school, she spends hours as she walks wondering what 'round shoulders' could possibly be. She takes the set-square from her pencil case and holds it against her body, the transparent plastic pointing outwards. How could a shoulder ever be square? Lucy pinches her flesh into a ridge. Still no right angle. For the photo, Lucy over-reacted to her mother's wrench, earning her a moment's collusion between her parents.

"Do you think she'll ever learn, or do you think she'll go on being a silly, stoopy, moony little girl all her life?" asked her mother in a stage whisper. Irritation thumped against Lucy's stomach walls with tiny fists.

" 'Fraid so," her father replies, "we're stuck with a saddy maddy little thing for a daughter."

The picture's still around somewhere. The people Lucy lives with still tease her about it, waving it above her head. Her flatmates, a man and a woman, are a fucking pain in the arse, and she can't wait to be shot of them. They pick up and throw her clothes at her, and shout at her when she leaves her cereal bowl out for more than two minutes. They give her a very hard time for shouting back, which for a quiet life she has finally decided not to do, but then she is obliged to listen to them shouting at night, in full earshot, fighting in a detailed and intimate manner. She has raised the issue at breakfast several times, but they are having none of it. They are nosy, rude, suspicious and hypocritical. However, they are also richer than her, thereby paying the rent and all the bills in this well-appointed maisonette to which they have all recently moved. They even throw in the food as well, so they've got her over a barrel, really.

And there are benefits to living with them. They are very good about making breakfast before she goes out in the morning, and the house is always tidy when she gets back at the end of the day. They have an OK washer-dryer, and a car. So, for a ten year old, Lucy is really very lucky.

"Lucynoddle, are you there?"

The coffee smells. Lucy drums obscure rhythms on her desk. A pool of milk, way below her on the road, disperses in the sunlight. The front door thumps shut. She feels the vibration four floors up, like a change in the air. She knows when people leave and enter the building, particularly all the people that come to see the woman who lives below them. Lucy is scared of this swarthy, gleamy woman and her glittering, constricting clothes, and her milk-throwing. Once the woman catches Lucy's eye on the stairs and smiles. But her parents have told her not to talk to the woman and so she hasn't, so far. But it won't last.

"Lucybeetle!"

Fuck off, thinks Lucy.

"Right well that's decided then. We're putting her on the Mininet and that's final!" For a building as well made as this, voices carry very easily up the stairs.

"How much will that cost, for God's sake?"

"I looked in the paper and it's only 80 quid a month. Seriously good value, in my view. And look, you can programme it to say the child's name, or a phrase of your choice, not just some bleep or something. We just download it down here, log her on – it's time she was anyway, I don't know what's wrong with her. All her friends have been posting away since they were three—"

"Bit of a baby, our Luce—"

"But there's always time to *change*—"

"Always time for a bit of a *change*," they sing in unison. The coffee burns. The dog barks, locked in a side room.

"And it'll save me screaming up the stairs." Lucy doesn't want to go on the Mininet. But she'll get it anyway.

Mr Towle is reading the paper.

"It's funny, isn't it darling, that when a child gets killed or abducted these days, they always wheel out a few people to go on about how she was a lovely little girl, had a smile for everyone, you know the sort of thing…"

"Lordy! Can you imagine what they'd make of it if our little Lucy got topped—"

"— or topped herself, hopefully—"

" 'Sour, stupid, ugly little girl who no-one liked anyway'—"

"— 'It's better she's gone,' that kind of thing. Ooh!" he puts his hand to his mouth, "actually that was a bit over the top."

"Imagine if some of those rough street kids got hold of her. She's had such a sheltered life she wouldn't stand a chance."

Once upon a time, people in the media talked about Future Shock. Then came computers for all, and science came out of the closet and got itself a popular makeover. But people soon got bored with ideas that would not be available to the human race for thousands of generations. Future Shock became Future Ennui. And so, parents could justify to themselves their disappointing offspring.

Mendel bred peas to prove the individual is not a pioneering free-range agent of will, but the logical outcome of a biological equation. Humans have a speculative freedom, when set next to the universe, akin to the spare space available inside a diving suit. That Mendel, a practising monk, should have taken such an interest in heredity is slightly mysterious.

At least Lucy's parents have not *created* her. She was the inevitable conclusion. Lucy is of normal height, appearance and intelligence for a girl her age. Her parents have not yet truly worked this through.

For her tenth birthday, Lucy got a camera.

"You only need your finger, darling! *Perhaps it'll stop her picking her nose,*" her mother added, loudly sotto voce. Her walls are soon covered with square pictures. Like all beginners at photography, she has tried earnestly to break rules she does not know exist, hoping that the seething beauty of the sun, seen through slit eyes as it moves slowly above a rooftop chimney, will somehow look the same on paper. The bleached, foggy results do not perturb Lucy. They are forms like any other, valid in shape and colour.

The Towles' home is full of luridly explicit Catholic art and reproduction heads of Michelangelo, only the most theatrically agonised, and the mother's very own specially commissioned, in distant, richer days, *Faceless Family*.

She looks, bored, at Lucy's latest effort.

"Not quite Annie Leibowitz, is it dear?" There is a major retrospective on at the moment.

"And whose is the little hand on the table in this one? Is it yours? Lucy! You funny little subversive!"

Lucy is not quite sure what this word means. However, her attempts at creativity do not go unrewarded. She is given a tick in the Towles' Life-Ledger, which will offset the forthcoming cut in her pocket money indicated by the cross in the opposite margin. Her last crime was to imitate the accent of a well-known working class comedian, whose programmes she is not allowed to watch precisely because she might do this. When her mother decided to set up the Ledger a year before, having got the idea from a satirical column in a Sunday paper, Lucy had one of her 'little dramas', for which she was instantly penalised. Were one of the teachers at Lucy's school to attempt such an exercise on a pupil, there would be an outcry, a lawsuit and a question in parliament.

Mrs Towle is fond of opera, putting it on whenever a difficult family situation arises. When Lucy does something wrong her mother comes after her with a small, dense, highly-powered portable CD player and runs with it banging against her leg as she hunts Lucy down.

Mr Towle is on the short side of average, with thin, but never actually thinning, dark blond hair. He has what some might have called a refined, even chiselled nose, creating for him a profile that sometimes causes women to look again. But when they do so they catch his eyes, which are too close together, and his mouth, which he always talks out of the side of, and soon feel his good points are really rather a waste. This realisation, however, leads to pity, which means they will at least chat to him. Mrs Towle is slightly too big, except for very thin ankles and wrists. Her pale hazel eyes are insecty-on-the-side-of-the-head, which worked in her youth but now makes her look insane, or as if there was room for a spare eye in the middle. She has an excessively square jaw, somewhere between the pins of which sits a mouth like an octopus beak which is sometimes smeared with coral-coloured lipstick.

Mr and Mrs Towle are somewhere on the electronic side of publishing, the proximity to creative or intellectual people justifying the banality of the work they actually do themselves. Certain levels of this profession are suitable for those who, like the Towles, have never felt *able* to be rich. Mrs is in visual media, while Mr sticks to literature, drawing the line at poetry. They watched both sets of parents burn briefly but brightly as small business people in the eighties, before going quietly downhill until the end of the century. Mrs Towle once enjoyed some status as the girlfriend of a well-known typeface guru before meeting Mr Towle, a more stable option. Mr Towle loves his text, and sits stubbornly with manuscripts when his peers are long gone into graphics. He also dabbles in antiques. Both always voted Conservative, but more recently changed to New Labour, much as one wheelchair-bound might cheer at a football match.

There might have been love there, certainly, which rose and claimed them in spite of the ethic of their upbringings. But now they stay together through another need. They had Lucy late, having tired of the chipped and fading widgets, for their kitchen, that they did not bother to replace. Their minds, never truly exercised by their work, seek a satisfaction that can only be gained through another, less experienced human.

"When I hear the word 'underground' I reach for my revolver. Don't you?"

"MORAL!" shouts the audience. "VIRTUOUS!"

Blood and sweat mix under the thin blue suit Reg is wearing for her debut performance. The audience below her are holed and scarred with piercings as if some minute fly-borne plague has picked at them and moved on. Reg thinks piercing is crap so her skin is laced with thin, but temporary, wires. During the performance she intends her suit to change from blue to purple, circles of red merging and flowering with her sweat. The dealers have been and gone. Only the back-up remains, a skinny little guy in white jeans.

The ceilings of the Depot are lost in blackness. Only the metal ridges of huge lamps can be seen, high in the dark. Outside, the December weather is damp, the usual disappointment. It is far too warm for snow and frost. The few scarves in the building are thin.

The audience is ranged around the space in the ring, enclosed by the far larger space of the Depot. The discernible odours here are hash, wine, something from Goa, a mix of perfume, the velvety vinegar of leather thongs, and the privileged no-hoper rotting on the vine. These people never change. Although colonialism in the British sense is gone, its cultural offspring, nearly sterile now from overproduction, are still hanging around, a race of the thin, the wealthy-by-default, the truly franchised. The MC steps out in front of them.

"Hey higher forces, get down here! This is the reeeeaal Underground! This is really *controversial!*" Expensive jeans squirm on the polished concrete. Signet rings move with a dull flash against the bloom of the night. In the brawny light, Regina's thick dark hair is shiny and densely moulded like astrakhan. Her skin is matte like suede. Some call her 'gipsy-looking'.

"Oh you literati and glitterati, you splendiferous arty-farty," intones the MC at the side, dark and subtle against a sea of largely white, "the unbelievable Regina brings you her art, 'er lovely art of gold!"

"Cold hard & yellow," murmurs a feverish looking woman in the front row, knees draped to the side, reluctant in her attraction to the vibe, and attempting to be dismissive of her own need to be here, at this space, at yet another performance. Her voice has a hectoring whine, her skin is foetally translucent, her mousy hair is mashed into a dull parody of dreadlocks. She has already had seven or eight abortions with semi-affectionate fathers, her mother secretly badgering the private doctor about her addictions.

"Little do we know the implications of this ritual," intones the MC, the sound of a saw on metal slowed a hundred times raking over the silence in the background. Art shouldn't need a commentary, and he sounds like something from the Tower of London or Madame Tussauds.

At a converted church in a similar part of London a similar event is going on. The creators of the art over there are more famous. More people are watching them than are watching Reg.

"We know what we think of this, don't we?" sneers Reg, taking a copy of *Style Bible of the Millennium* in which famous People of Culture have been asked what would be 'in' in the coming decades. She has already soaked it in petrol, and is now holding it in the air. She is sure she will excite the audience more than the previous act, an ironic juggler.

Reg glares at the posh folk below her. She holds one corner of the book's cover in her thumb and forefinger, the pages springing out in the spotlight. In her other hand is a burner. The flame's roar sounds distant, not small. The book looks suddenly important, framed by Reg's body, like a jewel floating before her. Reg lights the book and puts it down in front of her. The lights will be turned off as she does so, so that the audience are lit only by tiny safety bulbs, bleak china blue sonars far above.

Reg will put the flaming book down on a breeze block, go behind a screen, adjust the rotor blades in the baby's back, and with the sawing noise speeded up to a thrusting rhythm, send her sculpture, by way of a radio control unit, buzzing over the heads of the crowd. The skin around where the rotor has been inserted is bunched and frilly with sewing. The baby's eyes are glued open. Then a band, Zoot Stick, will do a live set, during which Reg will hand out flyers inviting the audience to a barbecue out the back.

"Beyond the limits of what is acceptable," the critics will say, canutes in the dusk by the pulsing ocean. But this may be their last opportunity. As Reg sends the baby into the air every spotlight in the Depot goes full on.

No-one knows what happened. No-one was near the switches. Reg pretends it was all part of the show but the fearful audience soon ups and leaves, the baby cruising overhead.

Somewhere far above them all, a page of unimaginable dimensions trembles in the infinitely massive hand of a reader who lets fall the book's cover, with its unfathomable acreage of hide, with a thunderous slap. Enough is enough.

After the show, Regina Voss, Manicurist of the Soul, as she billed herself for the show, takes her annoyingly camp friend Danny by the arm and rushes him home. Danny surfs on any art wave that comes his way. Reg is fairly into men at the moment, but just recently she hasn't really been into anybody properly. A light from the child's bedroom in the flat above hers still shines, although it is late. The mosque sounds the early prayer, sharp over their footsteps, the hiss and click at the end of the recording like a team of distant cashboxes.

As they close the front door, the preying screams of children can be heard behind them. Reg and Danny are fast and practised runners. This street's going to be unmanageable soon.

Reg, her hand firm as a money clip over the waistband of Danny's trousers, tows him up the stairs. They enter the flat.

Danny's chunky in a dark suit, but he's smaller than her.

"D'you think this is gonna work then?" asks Danny. "It's a helluva career change *now*, not that I'm being ageist or anything."

"What do you expect me to do? I'm going to be out of business soon, aren't I? You've seen the news, this fucking Human Genome Project thing is going to revolutionise the concept of personal growth for years to come.

"And anyway, I've always wanted to do this, to create something, to entertain people. All my life the only person I've ever entertained is myself. The only thing I've ever *created* is myself. And I don't want kids – imagine me with kids!"

"But Regina darling, I know you're trying to make a point, but a dead baby's a bit, well, *nineties*, innit?"

"No it's not! Not a souped-up flying one. Not a barbecued one."

"Yeah, but nobody stayed for that, did they? Somebody in there didn't like you. They fucked up your show. No-one wants to confront their innermost selves like that. It's too much. Even if they were all off their heads. It's too early for a retrospective, love."

Reg glares at him.

"You're not being very encouraging."

"OK then, how much money did you make tonight?"

"Some. Look Danny, I can't stand these manicured losers tripping in and out of my home any more. I can't take their stupid problems any more, and I've had enough of dreaming up fucking ludicrous treatments to sort them out. I'm not a therapist, I'm a charlatan. I always have been. It's getting stupid."

"Well listen to the lady!" Danny looks incredulous, "You get paid to fuck with peoples' minds, and some of them fall in love with you and keep coming back, and paying you. Sounds to me like you've had a fucking good one going for a fuck of a long time. You fucking love it!"

"I've had enough, Danny. I'll do a few more, just a few and then that's it."

"Yeah right, just one more hit. I've heard that one before."

Danny pours a glass of whisky and looks at Reg.

"I need a new start." A cat screams on the roof above. Danny walks over to the window and opens it.

A bar sign made of a huge pink triangle flashes two streets away, a pattern of little ones bopping around it in an endless conga.

"They wouldn't let me in there last night." Reg isn't listening. She is already planning what she will do the next day.

"Probably 'cos you're straight," she muses.

Danny slams the window shut. The slam has a bite to it, but the pane doesn't break.

"NO I'M FUCKING NOT!" he shouts, enraged.

"Coulda fooled me," she mumbles, raising the pitch of her voice.

"I'm not fucking straight," he murmurs, sidling up behind her. "I'm not. I'm bi. I always have been." He slots his arms around her waist, his broad muscular arms. He is smaller than her but strong as a monkey.

"Bitch!" He takes his jacket off and pushes her onto the bed. Reg is numb. This is just a game and the fire within her burns elsewhere. Part of her just wants to look out of the window. It's easier than looking at the past. She has done this so many times. Once, she nearly had her back broken by a couple of firemen on a rough night out. The end of October it was.

"Concentrate!" Danny squeals, meaning he needs to. Always from behind, to have sex on these nights is like playing a stack of school chairs for a GCSE photography project. She looks out of the window as Danny pushes into her. He's always so stiff, his cock like wood or metal, his thrusts fast and shallow like a cheque sorting machine.

Why do they play these games, she wonders. Is she cruel, or just pretending to be? Does she care? Danny, almost insensible in a lace-edged cut-away jerkin, comes in rapid fire. Thirty seconds later, Danny puts his jacket back on and leans out of the window again.

The city's luminous sweat, the light, draws into Reg. Below, the childrens' yawps are cut short. Up to now, Reg has so cleanly wiped the bottom of life's bowl that any darker imaginings about the reality of human nature would be irrelevant. But still, she might wonder why the press did not make more of her show.

The afternoon's short life is about to end. It is suddenly very cold outside, in the heart of mid-late December, when humans are warming themselves with end of year memories and have not yet begun the journey across the wastes of February and March. By the peaceful light of a dimmed TV screen, squat like a shrine in the corner, Regina is aware of her age, her well-worked fingers and the smoky blue veining that marbles the insides of her arms. The light outside turns to blue and orange. The doorbell rings.

Moving slowly, her clothing constricting her to the point of correction, she goes to the front door. The person has been let in downstairs without her knowing. Reg breathes deeply, her head wired and ringing. She doesn't believe she has arranged a consultation that evening.

Regina opens the door very slowly, hoping to intimidate her visitor into apologising and coming back another time. Whoever it is at the door will have been warned about her, but people can never quite be sure what they are being warned about. It is a caution on principle, as if referring to a poisonous plant.

Each client is so predictable, yet there is always some new banality or self-deception. Once a woman phoned Regina in desperation. Thinking that she had discovered a hitherto unknown suicide in the family, and was seeking reassurance, Regina instructed her to come over immediately. It turned out that the woman had decided one of her cats was autistic and wanted to know if it could be passed on to the children. And the speeches these women give; ones that they have given so many times before.

"…And you know, I've got such an addictive personality. I just have to have one gin, and then I just have to have another. I've been told I'm very, very needy, and that's why I always say no to sugar in tea, because if I have one I just won't be able to stop!"

But this one's different. Not a caffeine problem.

"So now I'm addicted to *not* wanting to see them and, every day, ten minutes before they all come out, I start shaking, and it's as if I actually need to not want to see them! Clever aren't I? I was always told I was clever, and often it's people like me who are addictive people, because our minds are working so fast that we just need to have more and more…"

"Them?" Reg bends in inquiry, slightly sardonic.

The door is pushed fully open, and in comes a flapping, fluttering woman, who keeps touching her face. Oh no, thinks

Reg, another one who has taken her emotional temperature once too many. Sure enough, the woman pulls out a small crystal and presses it into her forehead. After three seconds she looks at it and begins to babble.

"I knew I was slightly out of balance this morning but now I'm much, much worse. Perhaps I should come back another time. But it's 4 o'clock, there are so many of them out there, I just don't think I can handle it. I don't think I can handle it at all! Not at all! 8.30 in the morning and 4 o'clock in the afternoon. I can't go out! It's been a week now!

"And they run around in homeless gangs now, threatening people. It's disgusting!"

"Stop! Who are 'they'? Who's threatening you? What are you talking about?"

"Babies, children, they're all over the place."

This is a new one on Reg.

"What if I got pregnant?"

"You could always try re-absorbing the foetus, like mice and horses do when they feel threatened," counsels Reg, ever ready with a solution.

"The other night I dreamed I had turned into a cappuccino! My head was nothing but froth!"

Reg nods. Most people will never really understand themselves.

"Help me! I'm a Heritage Worker! I practically live on the streets! I've got people coming at me the whole time! Only a week ago two bloody hippies came up to me and anointed me on the head! I felt really funny for ages! And since then I've been going through all the stuff I just told you about. I've never felt this before. So much – hate."

Normally, at this point during a session, Reg might mention Seth – who, it must be remembered, was the one who quietly got on with founding the human race while Cain and Abel pranced about and got famous – and hold him up as a good example to those troubled by their lack of worldly success. But this is new.

Once upon a time, Reg was inspired by her work. She read history: the impact of the Industrial Revolution; the Reformation; the various plagues and wars. Further back to the invaders: Normans; Vikings; Jutes; Angles; and also the Romans – just off the boat and shivering with permanent sniffles, throwing up their hands, snorting and complaining that the locals smelt of what they ate. She topped up her learning with Freudian simplicities, taken from pocket editions. She considered those born in summer, for whom the cold of winter is a rude shock never forgotten, and those born in winter, for whom the arrival of summer is equally devastating. Those with very pale skins could well be descended from migrators, people who sought to push back boundaries and therefore, perhaps, did not have a lot of iron in their diet. Those whose ancestors did not have enough Vitamin A could not see so well, and would perhaps be more likely to live indoors, so therefore appreciate textures rather than views or colours. With serene flourishes, Regina painted pictures of what a person already was, and back and back for thousands of years, and what they would inevitably become if they did not change. Once, after a particularly sticky near-miss, she wrote a disclaimer. Any changes that occurred in a person's life after Reg had counselled them were not Regina's responsibility since, as she relentlessly reminded her clients, the human creature is infinitely changeable, and utter uncertainty about the future is what drives us onward. Anyone can change at any time.

She was lying, of course. Change in a human being is most unlikely unless fate takes the trouble to bend and poke a hole in the fragile persona he or she has been cultivating for a lifetime.

And now, her sympathy, professional and personal, has run out.

"Aside from suggesting that a dead cat boiled in olive oil, a medieval remedy, makes a very efficient gag, I'm not sure I can help you."

For once she tells the truth. The woman sucks a nail, and then asks cautiously, "Have you got anything for cellulite?"

Reg shows her the door and turns on the television.

...And now we move on to what you've all been waiting for...

Music accompanies the presenter as he pulls back curtains to reveal glittering charts, maps and bar-codes all swirling around together with flashing lights and strobes.

...This, folks, is you! Except, of course, I must tell you the display is slightly conceptualised just in case any of you see something different and wish to make a legal claim. (More music.) *This legal disclaimer was brought to you by Microsoft.*

To return to the point, from June 21st this year, you will be able to walk into your nearest pharmacy, offer up a tiny dab of your saliva and BINGO – your responsibility for your actions, and those of your dependents, is shelved!

But what will the completion of the Human Genome Project mean to you? No-one need ever moralise at you again about your life choices. You merely need to say, quietly, "Take a look at the lower part of my number 4 chromosome, and I think you'll understand." We'll all know which chromosome is which, and exactly what disease, character defect and unacceptable mental trait lies on each one. There will, quite literally, be no more mysteries! No need to get ripped off by expensive therapists either!...

Regina looks up and straight into his eyes, and realisation plunges across her sights like a bat. If she understands what the man is on about, soon we will all be able to tell, by the use of a simple test, which person is going to be a leader. Then we can put them in the fast stream and tell the other 19 out of 20 that they aren't going to become Prime Minister, so they don't have to bother. People will stop dragging themselves up the career ladder, and let the pushies swarm and squabble their way up there without regret, and without needing Reg. She starts to feel sick. She changes channel.

...And now, the weather. Freak conditions reported in the South East of England have been experienced yet again, this time by the residents of East Grinstead. A ten second shower of hailstones the size of cows demolished a community centre during a beginners Tai Chi class,

58 dead locusts were found in a telephone box, and giant sparrows have been spotted near a youth centre. These birds have a wing span of up to two feet. They are very aggressive and should not be approached. We'll inform you of any new developments as they arise...

Restless, Reg decides to go out. She always takes care where she goes, although she has scent-marked the whole city.

Out in the street, Reg braces herself to sidestep the relentless battle re-enactments being played out on the pavement. Ten yards down the street she is brusquely shoved by a burly roundhead reloading his musket. Further on, a Roman centurion is suffering himself to be kicked by a group of spitting washerwomen as plastic Sestertii spill out of his tunic and rattle onto the ground. Children dive for them before discarding them in disgust. An old man curses the scene. Heritage is in the air with increasing frequency.

But there's genuine tension on the streets as well. Two days ago, a man stabbed somebody to death in the fruit market. Even as the victim slid to the floor, the knife having made a clean entry, no-one took any notice, assuming a performance was taking place. Images of sudden death in the streets are fired so frequently at the public, from every visual medium that exists, that no-one goes to check if anything's actually wrong. Either a joke is being played on them in the manner of a candid camera production, or they are witness to some piece of art in the name of social comment. In this particular case, it was only when the killer began to stab himself, and his own blood to flow, that people became concerned. And even then there were doubts. Since then all street performers, even buskers, have been lying very low. So there is no music as Reg walks through the streets, thinking.

She hasn't read about herself yet. Maybe she misread the Zeitgeist. Maybe she did go too far with the baby. Maybe the press really is sick of artists and, having helped to create a culture where self-promoting monsters proliferate and talent gets left to wither on the vine, it's now revelling in its own backlash by ignoring everybody. Reg starts to feel foolish at the memory of her own performance. Look at her, a woman coming up to 40 prancing about in front of a load of druggies. For fuck's sake.

She tries to distract herself. The art of window-dressing is reaching critical mass. Shopfronts are protected by Clean Fortressing, giant liquid crystal plates, some translucent, some opaque with circulating images. No-one takes any chances with their frontage. With the newest material, if it shatters there remains an almost invisible lattice of carbon fibres inside it that would hold back an aeroplane. Only 'health' shops have resisted this, figuring, quite correctly, that individually washed mung beans and redoubtable, piss-like Kentish wine are not a burglar's highest priority, and even a whole warehouse of homeopathic aurum would only yield enough gold to cover the head of a pin.

Anyway, even if she wanted to go in and steal something, she won't get any further than the door, because it's half-day closing. The Village London scheme is starting to get on her nerves. Even corner shops have taken to it in earnest, as there is a special subsidy for those who let their shops lie fallow for a few hours a week. Cut-out parish pumps hang in the windows of participating establishments. Heraldry companies are burgeoning. A whale gules atop four Evinrudes rampant cost a prominent nature charity four and a half million to create and implement, but raises their profile unmeasurably. Bank façades are smaller and more intimate, the entrance doors creakier in front of all the noiseless steel and glass. The expression 'Counting House' is all over the place.

Reg walks for a while, barely seeing anything. She looks up and sees that a chemist is already advertising the forthcoming gene-testing service. The poster shows a family group all turned towards the mother and jovially making the sign of the cross as if to a vampire. *Your fault mum! Don't take it too hard!* they grin as one of the children is wheeled away on a gurney by a man with the word 'Specialist' pinned to his coat. Reg smokes.

When all human DNA has been logged and tabled, man's going to shout, "Ninety-nine, one hundred! WE'RE COMING!"

Then God will get up slowly, say, "Make my day, punks," and with a long-suffering sigh, hide himself under a whole new load of fresh viruses and evolutionary whimsy. Reg can't be the only one getting nervous. Two schools of thought prevail. One, that people will not need therapy any more when they know exactly what's wrong with them; the other, that people will be so traumatised by the truth of what they find out about themselves that they will redouble their efforts to get help. Money is already being made on the latter outcome, with many advertisements in glossy journals. Out of nowhere comes a voice.

"Could you possibly answer some questions for me? It will only take two minutes of your precious time."

A man, smaller than Regina and wearing a blue coat, is reaching out limply with thumb and forefinger as if to tug poignantly at her sleeve. In his other hand he holds a stopwatch. His thumb is poised over the button. He is a Heritage Worker. Regina usually snarls at these people, and sometimes jostles them, particularly if they approach her in a large empty space. But she knows that they are as keenly attuned to those who refuse to chat as those who take part willingly, so this time she stops. She cannot avoid his company. If only, she thinks, humans could crap, chat and eat on the wing like birds, eradicating all activities that take up time and space.

He pushes the button. His thumb is sallow-skinned and there is a white groove of long-standing in the soft pad.

"Gramercy for tarrying awhile!" His weary jocularity echoes dully, his white breath, though genuine, is like a cheesy Dickensian stage prop. He holds a voice-activated tape recorder, with bleeps to mark the beginning and end of each question. The legal ramifications have, allegedly, been ironed out. He sounds gentle but, due to his working alone, he could be armed.

"Do you consider England to have a great and illustrious heritage?"

"Occasionally," murmurs Reg, suspecting something about him. His voice is pale and soft, with a hoarse tinge from talking outside in winter.

"Are you aware that more than half the new inventions patented and manufactured in the world are of English origin?"

"Not surprised at all."

He has a delicate jaw, on the borders of weak, but saved by a flattish nose which balances it.

"Would you suggest to a foreign friend or relative that they come to live here in preference to their country of descent?" Large white clouds move overhead, patching one side of the street and then the other. Reg often suspects she is controlling the weather, but just recently it has not been doing anything she asks it to. She turns into the wind to warn off further questions, and walks. The wind and children squall on the periphery. Iridescent blue paint splatters in the gutter. She glares.

"Reggie!" He calls after her. No-one's called her that for years. A sharp cold touches her skin. But it is not the cold of winter but the sunless chill of a just uncovered corner of the past. She continues to walk.

"Regina, you remember me don't you? It's Luke!" Her breath is like smoke. She turns so that her body passes through it and faces him. Reg feels as if she is sliding on something. Suddenly it is not her feet going up and down, but the ground rising up to meet her. This time the bubble is bursting, the blister of memory.

"Luke! What the hell are you doing being a fucking Heritage Worker?"

Luke! She has fought so hard to forget the past, constructing a steel hymen in front of it. But now it is ruptured. Here is this little face, this little, earnest, nervous face, bringing it all back, blasting her barriers with one word, her own name, said in *his* voice.

Silently they go to the Ave Maria, a small dark bar half-way below ground, with deep red velvet plush on the walls and tiny silver offerings, hands, legs, eyes, entire lymphatic systems, pinned all over them. Varnished pietàs, stained with smoke, are positioned so that they glow in tiny spots of light. They go into one of the booths and sit down, each with a beer, on either side of a blackened wooden lattice. Reg stares at the flecks of gleam in his eyes. There is a silence over the murmur around them. The women at the next table shout at each other, then shush each other equally forcefully. Someone says something about 'disposal'.

"What's going on with you then?"

"Oh, the usual." Reg tries to give nothing away. What can you dare to give away after so many years? And talking through the screens always encourages a purity of fact she cannot afford to indulge in. And there is another noise she is catching above the whine of spinning years. Luke was once in love with her, and she can feel the sound of his love, across a perfumed room where they used to work together long ago, with swags of raspberry taffeta and chunks of gilded plaster. But she must talk.

"Actually, I've been a, well, sort of therapist for years, but recently I've been thinking of becoming an artist. Did you read about my show anywhere?"

She curses that last desperate little word even as it comes out of her mouth.

"No, I must admit I didn't, Reggie. An artist. How exciting!"

"Genetics is going to do us all in, Luke." She's aware of how mad that sounds. Genetics has been doing us all in since the day we were conceived and long before. But Luke looks as if he has other things on his mind.

"Reg, I never saw you after you burnt your books, or at least you said you were going to—"

They met at Diminuenda's, their first employer, 20 or so years ago in the early eighties. In vacations they worked as assistants (3.50 an hour) and part-time coffee table marblers (for which they got tipped in seafood) for a bossy teenage socialite with a caramel tan who sold antiquarian books to celebrities by the metre. Just Diminuenda was the name of the shop, everything touched with little gold stars and romanesque detailing. Similar women would come and go, flailing at each other with some newly discovered candlestick done by some 'sweet little man', or one of their own occasional tables made out of used plane tickets done in papier mâché. Reg would kneel silently, eyes lowered as she brushed, wondering how these people managed to survive when they had no blood in them. Reg's skills were not really any more valued than those of the fatiguer of ill-designed jeans, but her young boss was emoted and deceived by the apparent need in Regina, with her ember eyes, tarnished skin and swathed filaments of hair. Diminuenda, it seemed, was equally deceived by her own need to pity someone, and allowed her boyfriend to take Regina out, so she could see what a real South West London wine bar was like. Regina had already suspected this was not where the heart of the city was beating.

Reg smiles at the memory, although she does not feel like smiling. A woman brushes past their table, her face, pale and sweaty, averted from a table where two children in anoraks are having tea, apparently on their own. Regina shifts position on the pew she is sitting on, and remembers the long ago bar stools on which she listened to talk of weekends away in counties, and contact sports. Later on she sucked off the boyfriend with the same delicacy and strength that she put into Diminuenda's table tops. The man, red-sweatered, had never seen a deal gleam in a woman's eye like that. Regina, slim with survival, stole from her employer, particularly the little pots of perfumed gold leaf, and sold them on the side.

Soon after that, one evening in summer when she was 20, when the sunset was barbarous over a silent building site, Reg burnt her old college notes and textbooks. The memory is as clear as yesterday. The smoke began to race, faster and faster, from under the dense heap of papers; twigs crackled under the heap of bunched-up newspaper that supported the pile of books. Intellect consumed the rest of Regina's brain, not destroying but converting. The flames grew.

Sometimes it is important to burn books. Books only pretend they are the truth.

Reg left her old life behind, her old life of living along paths others expected her to follow. She knew she was 'different'. If she had not burnt her past, her path would have been dank and low, skirting rubbish heaps and disused caravans, as she was silted to silence under the rancid bullying of an office hierarchy whose higher echelons she knew she would never attain, positive discrimination or none.

She remembered a game she used to play as a child, and pulled papers from the piles, picking words at random: Vikings; Sagittarius; Vitamin D; full lips; earthbound. The collage of variants that make up every human being. These facts were no more than bricks, slips of interchangeable knowledge like matches in a model-maker's dream ship, but as she looked at them, she plotted. As she stood back from the fire, the steel struts of the building site were like a barcode against the sky. She must survive. She would become the best healer, the best alchemist of the heart, the world had ever known.

Reg was only too aware that everybody wants to *be something*. There is great pain in being part-something, not quite the whole thing; part black, part Jewish, part Scottish, bi-sexual, pied, mottled, a misfit. Those with the full complement are unforgiving. Reg, tortoiseshell through and through, knew this only too well, and could, she reckoned, with particularly heartfelt sincerity offer help to other humans.

She emptied the contents of her pockets into the flames, watched the dancing sparks, and considered her new career. Her decision grew and firmed as the chill of night built up behind her. After the fire died down, Reg looked and saw a tiny spiked component among the ashes, white and silver. The next day she met her first client, a crying lady she often saw in the street near her home. Reg befriended her.

"One of your ancestors probably married a wrong'un, so none of this is your fault!" Regina tried to look her in the eye.

It had to be the left one, as the woman's right one was so swollen that the cheek seemed to be trying to touch her brow.

"God loves homeopathically," Reg intoned. "A tiny dose of what He suffered will inoculate you against the realities of everyday life." Half the world, Reg would soon find out, was dying to find its roots, the other half to escape them forever.

That first night, so long ago, she dreamed a huge butterfly was fucking her, its legs jabbing her ready body like six foot hunting whips, the breeze from its massive wings picking up her hair, the iridescent powder from them trickling onto her body like cool sand. She had never dreamed like that in her whole life.

Luke's voice drones.

"—and then a few weeks after you left I saw you in the street wearing a wig and you walked straight past me." It costs Luke a lot to say that. He has spent so many years staring down at the dent in his heart.

"Did I? Oh, sorry." What can Reg say? How could she possibly have fallen in love with him? His emotions were too available to her. And anyway, she was in love with someone else and had not wanted to be worshipped.

When they met, Luke was trying to appease the memory of a very distant Brown Sahib ancestor who had eased the spiralling torment of a low to mid-level colonial administrator during the foul pre-monsoon months of a central Indian hellhole. Despite the slightness of this far-flung blood connection with another culture, he was proud to think of himself as the last remaining vestige of colonial guilt, being completely white. Working for Diminuenda further enhanced the ecstasy of his self-laceration.

Since then, his life has flickered from mild prosperity to the panicky edges of the middle class enclave. Reg listens to his story, which is similar to many, many others. In an age of enforced multi-skilling, he used to moonlight as a psychoanalyst, for which he was long trained but not really suited, not being sufficiently interested in getting power over other people. It was a shame, the analyst job paid well, but he simply did not have it in him to compete with the Gestalt-engineer and rebirther-fireman he shared an office with. Now he performs in Live Arts (Heritage), for which there is plenty of funding.

Reg orders a Guinness blended with fresh avocado and two egg yolks, the nearest thing to a proper meal she can bear. She will drink it and go. She has already had enough of him. She is pitiless because to pity others is to lay yourself open. There is a silence as the drink appears. He doesn't want to comment on it. He has not really changed. He's not capable of being up front about anything.

"But what are you going to do when your contracts stop coming? Heritage people only get weekly ones, don't you?"

"Well actually, I've been thinking about this. If I buy two hundred lottery tickets and re-sell them for 1.50 each to housebound old people who can't get to the shops, I'll have made a profit of a hundred quid! What do you reckon? If I did that every week, let's see, for 52 weeks, that's over five grand in profit! And if I—"

A glass smashes against the flagstones. Another dream crunched under the weight of its own senselessness and, like the bits of glass that get embedded in the soles of shoes and squeal over flooring, so the memory goes on humiliating. It's usually men, in times of trial, who have a particular need to set up ludicrous business schemes. His voice becomes reedily excited.

"I know, I'll put up some posters around the neighbourhood saying my mother will take in other women's piece-work – that's it! Respite for Home Workers! Luke Purvis, hero of the poor! It'll cost them next to nothing! I could take a night course in chick-venting and go and work for some Korean guy!"

Regina wants to hit him.

"I once tried to sell spent matches to model-makers. It seemed such a great idea at the time! I was going to do it in batches of two thousand! I must have dropped one on some newspapers while I was burning them. My auntie's got such fucking cheap armchairs, they should be fucking illegal by now. The next thing I knew I woke up coughing my guts out and the place was full of smoke! If I could only find a loan shark my problems would be over!"

He begins to cry.

"Regina, I've got to do something, the PSA are onto me." Several people at the bar look up with terrible pity. Luke's mother's arthritis is getting worse by the day, and she and his father are expecting to come and live with him. The Parental Support Agency brooks no complaint about bad interpersonal relationships or post-Freudian notions of personal space. Each PSA representative carries a mobile phone and a small computer, with which to input details about size of the living space in which the parents are proposed to be housed, the hours of work of the grown-up offspring, and their salaries. These facts are logged and subjected to an equation, which is transformed into a ratio, which will tell the reps how much money the offspring are obliged to spend on their parents or, in very few cases, how much the government will give them. "Extended families live together in other societies, and if they can, so can you!" the reps admonish, as the hearts of those they visit plummet at the thought of resurrecting so much buried horror.

"It's a fucking conspiracy!" says Luke. This man has been midwife to a glistening recollection, stories spinning in Reg's head. She should kill him for his alchemy of her lead-lined mind into the gold of old knowledge. Reg is distracted by her mobile vibrating against her. Her life is calling her away.

"Goodbye Luke," she says, "the world is no place for people like you and me." Of course, she means just Luke, but she cannot be so cruel now. He looks up. His features are radiant but the emotion behind them is pure, hysterical regret.

"Reggie, come and see me in the local council panto this afternoon. I'm playing a police cone!" Reg kisses the palm of her hand and makes a tossing motion.

Much later, after business, she turns on the news.

…just released details of a series of bizarre murders. This time, the victims were stuck to the ceiling of an office canteen in Hammersmith with notes attached. The victims have not been named, but are thought to have been from the increasing number of young people who are sleeping rough. Officers first at the scene, wearing protective clothing, said they had never seen such an adhesive. Samples of the glue are at this moment being tested, and a container was found bearing the logo of a unicorn…

Reg snorts at this concealed plug. A woman's voice comes on, soft, matter of fact, safe, suburban.

…You know how you feel when yet another bill comes in, and the landlord's getting strange men to come into the building, the building where you live, your home! He says they're doing the 'common parts', but how do you know that? And you go to a restaurant and they just won't serve you for ages. (Theatrical sigh.) *And you get your tax return forms and suddenly your heart feels low, so low, and you suddenly start to feel, well, afraid. I've been there, I know what it's like when your home is full of dirt because you just can't quite see the money for a cleaner, and maybe you feel bad about getting one anyway, and how will you pay the TV licence? And aren't you just a little bit sick of all those lonely bits of steamed broccoli and houmous on toast? Look, I've been there, I've tossed up between the lonely walk home late at night and a cab fare I just can't quite justify.* (Her voice softens intimately.) *Look! Do what I did. Just find someone and get married!…*

There is a tiny pause, before a gently insistent riff of Debussy takes the listener up and away into silence. A voice declares the previous advertisement to be a piece of copyrighted government property.

…and now, a brief memorial silence for this week's Lottery deaths. Oh, just a moment… a report has just come in of an orchestrated attack on a heritage panto currently playing on Chiswick roundabout. The lead traffic cone and half the chorus of underpants have been bludgeoned to death by representatives of a community action group calling itself the…

Reg knows it must be Luke who is dead. His pathetic attempts to forge a life for himself have been rewarded by the kindness of oblivion. He was too sweet, too malleable to cut through the undergrowth of human society. Reg jabs at the switch and knocks back a vodka, crying one tear which runs out of steam on her hot face. She thought she had buried the past, the way that famous actress had plastic surgery so as not to look like her dad, so the story went. But you cannot scrape memory from inside your face and head, it is there, running through you like mould, and far deeper.

If Reg's hearing were superhuman, she would have heard the stream of dull gunshots in the night.

Much later, she lies down to await her dreams. Soon she is in the forest, bent over, her head slammed against a tree, being fucked by an ape. Its slab nose is running, its hands steel brackets under pungent vinyl. On its first visit, it has familiar features, perhaps her own.

two

"WILD TURKEY STRAIGHT UP PLEASE," Reg orders a boy-type drink, guessing that the man she is meeting will be impressed by female assumption of masculine ways: gambling; football; types of beer; academic philosophy; fighting and really understanding animals.

She waits and waits. Two men appear at the bar near her, nattering slightly theatrically, a bit high. She has another drink. They are not dressed quite trendily enough. One of them nudges her arm, spills her drink and apologises.

"I'm really sorry! Let me get you another one." Reg has given up on her date and wants company. As if being directed in a film, they turn and scrutinise her face as she is drinking.

"Hold on a minute, you did that show the other day, didn't you! You're Regina!"

Reg is about to express flattered surprise, but they carry on talking.

"I'm Jamie and this is Phil. Wow, this really is a privilege!"

His accent flickers from street to common room and back again. They talk and then sit down. Soon, however, they become theatrically shifty, as if they have something to suggest to her. Reg's heart sinks. Please, no pills or dope, don't waste my time. Jamie speaks.

"You know, you were making some really strong points that night. You seem a real outlaw, someone who really likes to live on the edge!"

"Look," she says, "I'm too tired to talk now." She hopes they'll go away.

They are too pathetic, and too keen, to be drug dealers.

"D'you know, Regina, experts have calculated that soon it's going to be impossible to use any word, or combination of words, at all to denote illegal substances over the phone. Silences of different lengths are going to be the only option, and then those too are gonna get them on your case. And not a lot of people know that whenever the computer intercepts a drug call, it's instantly redirected to a call centre in Norfolk! Think about it — you're an ordinary punter, and you end up talking to Diss!"

They're trying it on, she is sure, but Reg doesn't want to go home yet.

"Jamie's just had his family logo done for his mum's Christmas present."

"Yeah right. A Vienetta couchant over two crossed Black and Deckers with a border of potato prints. They'll love it."

What appears from afar to be a sneer or, perhaps, a deformation of Jamie's upper lip after a fight, close up becomes a sheepish grin on one side of his mouth. He pulls at his earring affectedly, and strokes the panels of velvety hair that remain on each side of his head. In fact, he is quite sexy, with a wiry delicacy under the floppy exterior.

There is a short silence. They resume drinking, and talk about everything under the sun for the next two hours. Reg drinks fast. They seem to be keeping up well, although they won't let her go to the bar.

"Well," says Jamie, with student grandiosity over the comradely warmth, "I've peered into my soul's dank sweatshop and seen a roster with no name on it but my own."

"You see Regina, you look like one of us, so frankly I'll tell you that things have been a bit complicated since we left our jobs."

"You see, we're doctors. You wouldn't believe it, would you!"

"But we couldn't take any more. What's left of the NHS is lies and bullshit. You can't treat anyone who's ever done anything in their life at all – smoking, drinking, drugs, the lot. All that are left are monks and librarians, and not many of those either. The rest have to pay. It's sick."

Jamie's eyes are fuzzy now.

"And the pharmaceutical companies, they're the sickest of all. They spend millions developing a new drug, and then they decide that it's going to be too cost effective—"

"Like light bulbs, or tights."

"Yeah, just like light bulbs, so they do something to it so that it doesn't work so well. Or they just don't patent it and let it sit there in the warehouse.

"That's barking mad," says Reg.

"My conscience won't stand it," says Phil.

"But we need money, like we all do, so we tried to do something on our own."

"Something a bit more – underground."

Reg's heart sinks.

"Let's just say we've been overdoing it on certain fronts. Why do you think it says o/d on your bank statement, har har?"

"I mean Regina, like I said, you look like one of us!"

Jamie pulls into the conversation like a van down a clear slip-road in the middle of the night.

"You could say, Reg, that we got ourselves a sort of revolving credit facility with a difference."

"Yeah," says Jamie, "the dosh goes into valium first, and then legs it out of there back into cash—"

"It went into coke for a bit after the August bank holiday blizzard, then out again after the hold-up at Colchester—"

"Then into belts—"

"Belts?"

"Yeah, a load of those kids' ones, Steel whatsit, you know, from the cartoon, we did right well out of that—"

"Then back into money again, then into Valium for a while—"

"Yeah, all right, all right—"

"And all I can say is," says Jamie, kneading at the bar with his hands, like a kitten looking for a nipple, "that the rich get richer and the poor get poorer—"

"And the rest of us get strung out in the middle like a chain of rotting peas." Phil's voice is quiet.

"Anyone for a government necklacing?" asks Jamie, a bit too loudly.

Reg takes a drink. They really are just a couple of fucking students wasting her time.

"Are you going to do any more shows, Regina?"

"Well, maybe, but it all costs money."

The boys look at each other for a split second.

"Well," says Jamie, "when you see what we've got here, it's probably best you keep a low profile from now, know what I mean?"

Reg gives a practised sceptical look. Phil rubs his pocket and shivers, although it is getting very hot in the bar.

"This is new, Reg, we only got hold of it last week—"

"We've got a bent rep working for us—"

"Never seen anything like it." A coppery glittercube twists above them, dappling their faces and Phil's bald head.

"Basically, it was going to be pills, but it's sort of like an ointment, and it's basically like a sort of herbal chill-out drug but with pretty pictures to go with it. Sort of bends time a bit, too."

"Bends time, that's the first time I've heard it called that," laughs Reg.

"Um, think of it as a, er, kind of skunk jelly, but it's nothing to do with cannabis—"

"I think it originated in, er, South America or something."

"So, have you tried it then?"

The music gets much louder. Reg is trying to make out what Jamie is saying.

Reg half rubs, half snaps her fingers.

"Reg, we'd like you to get first look at this because if we give it to Pete 'n' Rob Wolf, like we usually do, they'll bleed us dry!"

Reg lurches at the thought of those overpromoted twats getting hold of anything before her, let alone a new drug.

A tiny, dark man suddenly appears with a miniature sandwich board covered in earrings.

"Wanna lose weight, lady? See the tiny magnets that hold 'em, they're like acupunk, you know, make you not eat!"

The earrings are cheap, with a slightly mis-moulded plastic pearl in each, badly glued. The magnets are tiny.

"So show me what you've got then."

They go on talking while she pretends to look at them.

"Phil."

"Yeah?"

"D'you think Chardonnay's become a meme?"

"Wot?"

"Well, I'm wondering if society's caught on to the social and commercial implications of a type of grape that's demographically egalitarian, you know, spread all over the world, like. And they're not liking it. Obviously that's a paradox, but a unit of cultural inheritance can be negative as well as positive, you know."

"Come on, what've you got?" says Reg.

"You've got to check it out now, 'cos I'm straight on the phone to Pete 'n' Rob if you don't."

The hectoring tone in Jamie's voice is practised, but not that good. Reg is drunk and wants some excitement. She knows that in some ways her urge to try something new at her age is a sign of weakness, a sign of unwillingness to plough her own patch properly. The boys seem heedless of her again.

"If you measure a drug in terms of its half-life, Phil, then surely it's never gonna leave the body. The host organism is doomed to retain traces of it, however fractally infinite."

"If you say so, Jamie. I still think that the other X cannot be reactivated—"

"You mean you can't get your last girlfriend but one to shag you—"

"Well, if she won't, she won't."

Reg stares briefly at the football on the screen behind the bar. Customers for the virtual game are trooping dully out of a backroom, rubbing their eyes and hair. The highlights come on.

The lights in the place flicker on and off.

"When that happens I always think God's come by for a quick half. Just letting us know he's one of the gang."

"So have you got it here?" Reg asks.

"No, that's the point, you'll have to come back to our place."

Somehow she is reassured by their demeanour. Whatever it is they are up to, she is sure it is not rape, or murder.

"Where are we going?"

"We could walk but we'll take a cab. You've got to watch out for that lot on the corner of Edgware Road, they're right nasty. All under eight years old I'm told. They look 15 though. Fuck knows what they're putting in kid's food nowadays. It's funny though, 'cos the ones actually wearing school uniform are docile as fuck most of the time…"

Phil and Jamie's flat is hung with steel casts of Habitat-style Chinese paper lanterns which turn slowly. They sit down on an appliquéd sofa. Jamie disappears and returns with a tiny pot. He dips his finger in and wipes it on her forehead.

"You know where you can stick your Tiger Balm you hippy trash!"

"Chill out, wait a second or two."

Reg lies back. Perhaps she is being filmed. She soon stops caring. Within minutes she is spinning inside a centrifuge of thoughts hued with golden light, leaving her earthly body heavy, precious. It is as if the skin of her eyeballs has been plucked up, painlessly, and stretched for thousands of miles, taking her mind with it. She gets up and tries to walk. A harmless half-eaten doughnut left on a plate on the coffee table is transformed into a pungently erotic Spanish-style tooled leather pouffe, hawking itself suggestively by the fireside. There is a sound like a telephone, but the small black handset does not look capable of producing this otherworldly strum. It's just like in the HG Wells story about the men who defied gravity, jumped out of the window and ran around people while they moved like dying derricks, the obscene wink of an old man rendered even more uncannily repulsive. The strum calls out again, the sound coming at her like a leather belt cracked in syrup. She walks around. If the boys are whispering, the sound has flattened to something like ten thousand people blowing rhythmically into oil drums at the bottom of a well. She looks at them. Their faces are frozen in fascination *and* something else. Phil is reaching for something. She slews across the room. Her hearing is magnified, yawed. From behind a door is a sound of glass-on-glass, a tiny noise like grains of sand nudging each other. She opens the door and sees a microscope. On it is a slide which is sticky with a dark, honey-like substance which is growing and heaving itself onwards and downwards from the slide with the delicate slowness of rising dough. The smell has a bitter sweetness. She is dreaming about a laboratory. It has a mouth which seems to be telling her to do something. She senses a touch on her shoulders which increases until she is forced to sit again, and then lie down.

When she comes round, there is a small flash of white in front of her, and Phil hands her a cup of tea.

"I had a dream about a laboratory. What do you call that stuff?"

"We're not sure yet. D'you want some more? That was on the house, of course."

Two weeks later, Reg has made 13 clients very happy.

There is a chord from the computer. Reg goes over to the screen to see who is trying to contact her. A few have since her show, some to abuse her, some demanding to work with her. She does not reply to any of them. She's been thinking too much recently.

She looks at her new messages and for a moment wonders why no-one has yet given the reshuffling of *qwerty* any serious enthusiasm. The easiest word to write on a traditional keyboard is still 'property'.

She has received a genderless email. She gets pissed off before even bothering to try and work out who sent it. God, the number of 'Mick's' and 'Zoltan's' that turn out to be brooch-wearing, card-carrying females – who are they trying to kid? Her days of shouting at computers are long gone. She had campaigned against them, when she was a student, off her face, bursting into people's rooms with Luke right behind her, screaming at the sagging necks and shoulders, cricked by the shocked upturning of heads, "You're all killing yourselves!" and pouring beer into the keyboards. It got her an interview on hospital radio and a mention in a *Guardian* piece about the New Student Radicalism. But it was held against her in the long run.

Regina dosses around with the keyboard, cramming food into her mouth without looking at what she's eating. Usually, she knows something's up when she cannot even be bothered to cook. She waters the plants and wipes their soft silent leaves. The blurred chord echoes again.

Regina. I'm around. I need you. Remember what I did for you.

Fuck's sake. So it *is* another bloody admirer. And this one's alleging there's already been something between them. Yet another one who wants something from her. She ought to be pleased, but she isn't. Reg feels like St Francis of bloody Assisi. Mind you, what a con he was. He smeared himself with honey, and hid cheese and raw steak in his pockets, that was what caused the holy swarming.

Yeah, yeah, *Remember me*. These crushes are going to start pissing her off very, very soon. It'll be some ex-client who's still got one of Reg's old nail clippings in her secret box. No-one has actually cloned an entire human, taken a cutting from a person and regrown them out the back somewhere, at least no-one she's heard of, but it won't be long now. One or two doomed lovers seemed to take more away with them than just a memory. Someone jogged her once while she was chopping some garlic, "Let me watch you." The knife flew into her finger, and he was a little over-attentive in his application of Dettol. The captured pixel of skin left a dent behind it. "Hair's bad, teeth are worse, but don't ever let anyone get their hands on your skin!" a greying, dreadlocked friend of hers once counselled, nodding over his thesis.

The room is dark around her. She is lit by the milky light of the screen, like a damp blue blush in the black air. As a young adult she could see where others cursed the gloom and sat in buff pools of lamp-light or under crushing fluorescent tubes. People sometimes commented on this, and she would make a remark about her liver-eating ancestors, that carrots were merely a garnish when it came to eyesight, and perhaps she was descended from cannibals. She coughs. This is new. Tobacco usually makes her mind move like a mandrake, its roots rippling over the ground. She's been coughing too often. She decides to go to evening surgery. She can pay.

The doctor is a pleasant young man who idly taps a ruler against the creamy tips of his slightly too long nails. He explains to her that only those as intelligent as she is are capable of comprehending the plot between cigarette manufacturers and the powerful, to slow down everyone to the speed of plant life. If left unchecked by smoke, intelligence spreads through the mind like a virus, consuming emotions and empathies as the smoke consumed oxygen, energy and volition.

At the end of the visit the doctor adds, edgy, casually, "Of course, if you continue to smoke after September the first next year, it's possible you will be denied treatment for all illnesses, smoking-related or not."

His hair is the colour and consistency of bacon rind, pasted smooth over his broad head. He says, "Oh, and you weren't intending to have children in the near future, were you?"

"No, definitely not."

"If there's anything wrong with you, you know, anywhere, they find it sooner or later." Then, he tentatively inquires, "How do you feel about children in general?" She shrugs.

She goes home and coughs some more. The air is thickening, as if in preparation for something.

The bell rings. It's a client who popped in a week ago for almost no reason, just to chat. Reg prescribed the ointment and that was that.

"Regina, I'm back."

"So I see." Christ, so she threw up a few times, so what?

"It's just that I needed to see you again. Well, since I last came, things have been a bit odd, and well, would you treat me again?"

"Didn't that stuff I gave you help? Do you want some more?"

"Oh yes it did, but I've got plenty left. No, I've been thinking a lot about – well, life." Reg groans inside. She indicates the couch.

The woman lies down and Reg looms over her. She feels the heaviness of her own skin, or guilt, dragging her downwards. The therapy begins.

"What an old soul! A very, very old soul!" Regina sometimes finds her own coyness unbearable. "Tell me your *best* dream."

The woman tells her about being on a sledge, but going uphill with her hair flying forwards. Huge hunting horns reached up, transformed themselves and pierced her. Reg wants to hand the woman a crystal goblet full of a bubbling purple murk and say, "Drink this."

"Drink this," she says, handing her new client a small cup of coffee. "Maybe you want to get your genes tested? You don't need to, you know. I can see your good nature all the way back to the Cretaceous! You've got some Viking in you, it's the ears. Don't be misled by your dark hair, though there is obviously some Celt in you too!" The woman looks slightly depressed. She sounds hollow, as if her head is in a bucket.

"It's children, you see. Children! Their hard little faces! Their vast cash withdrawals! Suddenly all this has come home to me in the past week, since I last saw you. I've realised how much I hate them."

Regina puts the tips of her fingers together and pushes firmly. The tendons bulge beneath the skin. This woman has been watching too many TV programmes.

"Did you know many other children as a child? Have you had problems relating to them since?" The visitor warms up.

"Well, that's the point, it was when my sister had her two that it began," she replies. "And the thing is, obviously my sister's not married or anything, and there's a strong possibility the little ones'll have to go into a Care Community. And I feel so guilty because I'll be so pleased when they do! In fact, I've already made one tiny little call to the relevant person, if you see what I mean. I'm so naughty!"

"Could it be that your mother communicated this to you, that your ability to imagine life as a separate being has left you in a profound state of unease as to the very nature of your individuality? There can be no life if you yourself see yourself as a dead end, a self-consuming artifact, a sterile—"

"When I see a child in the street I start to shake, my hands go all clammy and I—"

Reg cuts her off with a wise raising of her hands, palm outwards.

"God couldn't destroy for you, so you must play his part. Perhaps you would like—" The woman seems dangerously biddable. Once on top of her, Reg continues to speak.

"I am your mother. Once you have lain with me intimately we can separate and you can live out your real life in glory. Two nurturers, two containers cannot contain each other! We are not a set of magic balls carved by Buddhist monks! Look, I'll show you." The woman's eyes are wide with surprise, or horror, or even welcome. Reg unzips her dress, pulls it up and presses against her client, her hair bursting from its clasps and sheathing the woman's sight from what is happening to her.

"I'm your mother, I'm your mother! Sit down, darling, and get on with your sponge cake!" Reg uncases and offers a breast, still fine though the upper skin is becoming papery over the faint mauve lines that span it.

"Take me back, then spit me out!" she exhorts, calmly. Reg begins to rock against her, all the time thinking about the period photographs and drawings she will pull out and show her visitor to see if she would like to spot the age she thinks she might be reincarnated from. Discreetly Reg observes the physiognomy below her. Empire line would probably suit her best, with her strange shoulders like the ones in a Turner drawing. The harder Reg looks, the more repulsive the unnatural slope of them becomes. But her client has a good jaw and broad cheeks and will, therefore, carry the correct hairstyle. She imagines the two of them in a carriage, perhaps a brougham with a chestnut pony, flowing past brambles along a country road, larks singing high above. Reg prays her client has no fantasies of having been Nefertiti or suchlike. The picture has got so dog-eared. She could have scanned them all onto disc ages ago, but the physical object is better for evoking the past.

"And here's my very own Hand of Glory, to protect and oversee!" says Reg, joyously. She flexes her own large hand before it swoops with colloquial grace down between their clothes and onto her client's hot, filmy vulva, walking this Lilliput landscape for several minutes until the woman comes in spite of herself. Her hands, still cold from the day, grip Reg's shoulders with the slight shock. The skin on her calves and shins is powdery through her tights, from the cold outside. A tiny flush rises in her cheeks.

"Do you feel better now?" The woman can hardly deny it. Reg feels simultaneously young and ancient, as if she is dancing on some sun-flattened hilltop way south with a tinny, atonal church bell sounding against the dessicated hills. She imagines corrupting nuns, her cowled seductees rippling and folding before her as if arranged by an unseen hand. The woman sits up.

"Two students selling things from the rainforest sold me some lip balm the other day. It was really weird. It was just like your ointmenty stuff."

Reg is feeling vicious now; for her, animals, children and the mentally ill provide the best company, while the perturbed sane, who pay for her advice and relief, are just fucking irritating. There is more to be learned from alternative minds, and more to be taken.

With her fee, the woman leaves something large, round and flat wrapped in a plastic bag. Reg hopes against hope it's a dartboard, but no, it's a fucking camembert. She spits in disgust, goes to the kitchen and puts on a surgical glove.

Reg has a horror of dairy products. She tripped and fell into a bowl of milk when she was a toddler on a visit to a farm and has never forgotten the warm thick liquid cowl that cling-wrapped her and pooled in her where it could. Stuff from a cow's insides! Puke! And she read once that rat's milk was nearer to humans' than cows', anyway. If she ever finds a pint of milk in the hallway she turns her head disgustedly to the side, picks up the carton between thumb and forefinger, carries it delicately down the stairs and hurls it back out into the street, enjoying watching the carton explode, the white seeping silver to grey on the tarmac and slowly disappearing. Reg always wonders why Christian campaigners have never cottoned onto milk as an offering instead of all the bread and wine palaver. Its paleness and off taste perfectly match the religious education lessons of her childhood: the crappy singing; the puling morality; the colouring in pictures of Paul of Tarsus; the videos about abortion with their slightly 'anti' stance without being explicit, and slides of cancers, the breast tumour like half a fried tomato laid in the armpit. The memory entrances her momentarily like a good music video. The memory is fresh, like a film. She hurls the cheese out of the window, spinning it so it leaps briefly in its box and crumps to earth.

As the cheese spins, Reg imagines every cell in her chanting its minute instruction. Why do scientists have to mess with everything? The scientists play God, as she herself has played God with her own past, trying to redesign something already designed. Mapping the genome isn't going to solve everything.

But as the cheese spins downwards she has an idea. She looks through the library books on the table. She reads about the much discredited Jean-Baptiste Lamarck, best known for his theory that acquired characteristics will eventually worm their way into the body and become inherited. Thus a philanthropic strain in a city father may emerge two or three generations later as a natural generosity of spirit and a desire to help others which may, if fortune staggers, transmute into a gruesome and entirely unwanted need to get involved in other peoples' business. Reg is not sure where she stands on Lamarck. Wasn't it memes that he was on about?

To relax she listens to a batch of dead noises she got at a car boot sale the other day: a needle on a record's final groove slowed down so it resembles ancient breathing; the thud of a hardback book thrown onto a table, speeded to purring; the minute splash of the extinct raft spider kicking off from a pond's edge; the whirr of a milk float, which fills her with horror and disgust. She likes the book best. As the sound speeds up, Reg's idea grows and mutates.

The World's First Exhibition of Genetic Poetry! The greatest scientific satire since Prozac! by Regina, Reaper of Truth!

The air is knife sharp through the open window, the low winter sun like a doctor's lamp between her eyes. Her breath burns with cold but still she leaves the window open.

45

You can only be a nobody for so long. She grabs for the *Yellow Pages* and gets going. For two hours she talks and haggles and cajoles advice and orders goods, from suppliers, builders and pet shops.

Later, Regina sits under the gold and lilac evening sky. I could be God, she thinks. Her head is a vast cube of eyes. She was not born but created, a divine prototype. There is only one person and that is me. She feels much larger than her surroundings. If she tries to stand she will find the roof of the building resting on her shoulders.

There is a noise upstairs from the flat above. That poor little girl. There is a sound of a woman running in the street below. Low heeled court shoes in need of reheeling. Little feet behind her. Reg goes on working. Three clients come, all repeats of the cheese-woman. All loved the drug she gave them, all now detest children. It's as if she has hypnotised them. But she does not care about business any more. There was probably some article in the paper about motherhood being bad for you or something. The phone bellows.

"Reg? Reg! Wake up, it's me, Lou. I left you loads of messages. Is everything all right?" The voice giggles, seeming to shower Reg with entitlement, "Of course you remember me."

Is it the one who wanted to clean for her? Just clean, unstoppably. She recurred and recurred. But it doesn't sound like that one. And the expectant silence when the woman on the line stops talking almost immediately fills with a long lost violent image. Reg's love of experiment was not shared by certain of her teachers and contemporaries. Disappointingly, the people in power did not want to use her talents. The only person who'd been impressed had been a bloke called Joe, who nodded and grinned and asked her to join him.

"Reg are you there? Reg I need you!" The female voice is more singsong than 20 years before. "You *do* remember me. Oh let me come round!"

Reg begins to realise but doesn't really believe who is calling her. She would have expected the rich, confident and slightly cynical tones of a woman lawyer who made it against many odds, who had become muscular in body and intellect after a career of such weight, and finally, heavy with accolades, a stateswoman above the petty world, was being profiled in magazines for no particular reason except her stature. But the voice she hears is squeakier, more urgently space-filling. It sounds like a child's, which is strange because its owner is at least 15 years older than Reg.

The new arrival is wearing a fawn trouser suit and a smiley T-shirt. The hair is a madwoman's henna-and-grey. It's Lou, the lawyer who made her name on Reg, who saved her. She has had many facelifts and is decorated with discreet implants. She is shaking.

"I saw one on the stairs! It just stood there and looked at me!"

Lou puts her hand up to her face. She is in her early fifties. Her face is broad and angular but the stylishness of its essential masculinity is spoilt by the make-up; the lipstick a little too pink, the make-up a little too orange against the hair, the eyeshadow a little too blue, altogether giving the impression of a doll pumped up and left to weather outside. Her shoulders are heavy, her coat is thick. Lou sits down with a slight simper.

To calm herself down, Reg switches on her murals which play against one wall. The murals come with sounds in a batch with three options: primeval ferns waving gracefully against a smoky backdrop of volcanic exhalation; crowds of delicate lemon-yellow bacteria flitting in a garnet-hued undersea, and a close-up of a pan of boiling milk, played backwards and forwards as if breathing. Lou sits down. Tiny spitfires fly past the window. The children across the courtyard are playing Second World War.

"Lou, it's been so long. What are you doing here?"

"Reggie, you were always so selfish! Treat me! Treat me now! Don't think I don't know what you've been up to!" It is as if the woman has been away for two weeks, not 25 years.

Lou won a landmark medical case on Reg's behalf when Reg was little and, in doing so, launched her own career, as well as providing Regina with some money when her family died. Regina's mother did not know what was happening even before they discovered little Regina's birth defect. After the case, Lou was fêted in the press and spent several years taking up cases like the one where a mother sued her grown-up son for the damage he had inflicted on her vagina at birth. Lou made her career on Reg. Reg has a flashback to herself fidgeting with a doll as the papers were read and re-read, and what to say explained, in that mortuary courtroom. Reg wants to be alone with the memory, not shouldering social obligations.

But Lou bosses her out of the way and lies down.

"Let's dispense with the niceties. I'm going mad! I can't stop dreaming about maggots. Maggots in my pockets, maggots when I open food to eat it, maggots in my bag when I look for my keys. The maggots, they are crawling towards my, my vagina! What does it mean, Reggie?"

Reg stalls, bemused. It is like a dream. First Luke, now Lou.

"Remember, the best way into a woman's stomach is through her heart."

Lou ignores her.

"But you know, what's strange is, once these maggots have got some way in there, they all turn round and start pouring out again! And then I saw one on the stairs just now! I say to myself, who left this fucking thing there? Like the ones I see every fucking day."

The word is harsh coming from her mouth.

"The sky could crack open, Regina, and more of them could fall out of there. What's happening to me? It's just been over the last couple of weeks. They're everywhere I look, in singles, pairs and groups, waiting for me, making their noises all around me, like little – little slips of hell! Living splinters waiting to stab my flesh!"

Bored and sickened, Reg longs to know what Lou is doing here. She feels tired and irritable.

"Lou," says Regina, "you do a lot of work outside and have a horror of maggots which are, of course, worms by another name, and represent to you nature's ingratitude and great power. You do all this pruning and clipping and pushing seeds into the ground, and yet the one thing you do not want from all this is a soft pink creature resembling more a part of you than a rose or sweetpea. You see, this is Mother Nature's way of saying, 'We are not so far from each other – how dare you presume to mother me!' But you're forgetting that worms are actually benevolent, and maggots are merely the gentle bureaucrats of Death. Worms are hermaphrodite, tidy, clean creatures which do not leave waste behind them, physical or emotional.

"You were born under the thirteenth sign, the sign of the Lido. An interesting tripartite sign, this one. First of all, it's a man-made pleasure-pool buried in earth; but then it is full of water; and then it is exposed totally to the air! So you see what a versatile sign it is, too. The fire, however, which so much seems to drive you, is from unwelcome influences such as the pollution an ancestor of yours must have experienced while helping start the industrial revolution. Do you see penises there at all?" Usually, at this point, a look of light revelation comes over the faces of her clients. *Ah yes, I see what you mean.* If in doubt, pull out a dick. But Lou is looking at Regina with utter disgust.

"My God! It's taken me this long to track you down. Regina, after all we went through! I saved your life, have you forgotten? I'm not some bloody gardener racked with guilt at my superiority over a bunch of fucking cabbages! You stupid girl, I'm talking about children! It's children I am afraid of, little children! I saw one on the stairs. It nearly killed me!"

"Oh. That must have been Lucy."

"The last thing I want is its name."

The patronising weariness in Lou's voice is too much.

"Fuck you! Fuck you, you snotty bitch, barging into my life like the last 30 years never happened! I charge for my time, you privileged cow!"

Reg's anger is grief too, like a child's. She slams her hand on the couch.

"Sorry, sorry, sorry. It's just that I overheard someone talking about someone who just had to be you, and I tracked you down."

Lou the lawyer, Lou who was a sort of substitute mother to Reg, is irritable but under that is terror. Fear makes myths, thinks Reg; the myth of what might be there, all constructed in a nanosecond. Lou leans forward.

"Have you had any children of your own?" asks Reg.

"No, but now everything's about to change!"

Suddenly, with the word 'change', Lou's whole demeanour resets itself. Her voice takes on an awful intimacy, her face becomes taut with sentimentality.

"Regina! I had to see you to tell you about the little surprise growing inside me!"

"Oh, Lou, congratulations! How lovely for you!"

"I was surprised at the doctor's hostility towards me but, of course, it was all his problem, nasty little man – but it's in us all! I say that I believe in compassion for all living beings, and especially for my impending little arrival! But now I've got this thingy where every time I see a child in the street I feel sick! What am I going to do?"

Lou is being punished for her earlier lifestyle. While unexceptional at the time, it has come back to haunt her now she is pregnant. She, like all other lawyers, smoked, drank and took a lot of drugs.

"And now I should really be in hospital but they won't let me because I was a bit naughty when I was young. The point is, Reggie, the doctor told me that if I got some old silver napkin rings or something then I could barter them for treatment and it would actually work out a hell of a lot cheaper than paying up front."

Reg assumes Lou is replete with hallmarked bits and pieces, given her origins. When she was visiting Reg as a child, she would get out a silver coke spoon she'd had made in India and remark darkly about its powers.

"Oh Reggie, I gave everything to Johnny! He needs them to sell for his tours around the world. Everyone's given loads of stuff to him."

"Who's he?"

"Johnny? Oh, he's wonderful!"

Lou is not a lawyer any more. Her career changed the day she had to defend a self-help guru who was being accused by a reluctantly addicted but increasingly impecunious detractor. A week after she got him off, Lou threw in the towel at her chambers and became her new master's private advisor, recruiting minor celebrities to bestow specious glamour on his advice.

Most of her subsequent conversation is based around what a kind and loving person her employer is, as is she. Regina has met a lot of people like this in the course of her career. The guru does not pay very much, so Lou is up shit creek financially.

Funny how no-one talks about rights any more. It's all about fitting in. Reg looks out at an old man in the street. Inching on spread shoes, he takes ten minutes to pass in and out of her vision. She is so absorbed in his progress that her cigarette burns all the way down. She barely jumps at the pain.

"Reggie, what are you going to do about these women who've been going around attacking children? I've heard right, haven't I? Surely you can help them or something."

"I can't take responsibility for everybody in the entire world. I'm not the social services!" Reg snaps.

"But I mean, they're going to go to jail if they get caught, and be charged with acting on perfectly normal feelings which I understand totally."

Reg looks at her.

"I want to help them myself, but I've not been feeling very well. Of course, human love is infinite… which is why Johnny's so amazing! But you know, it was funny. A mad sort of hippy person was dancing around waving beads and sticking his finger in people's faces and anointing them with something, like in India. And he did it to me and I felt really good for a while.

And I thought, that's just me accepting that poor man for what he is, and that's my inner love coming out!"

Upstairs, Mrs Towle is contemplating the conversation she has just had with a cowled, raisin-fingered creature outside by the bins in the rain. The creature has seen how Mrs Towle feels about her own child, and has made suggestions towards the bigger picture.

In her bedroom, Lucy notices that when she pushes her fingers together in a church-shape, there is a hum. Perhaps inside her own head. She smiles.

three

"TEN YEARS OLD AND DRAWING WITH HER FISTS! Perhaps she's retarded," the visiting governor murmurs to the art teacher. The teacher frowns carefully.

"We don't discriminate here, and she's fairly new. But at least she's quiet in class."

"Well they all are these days, aren't they?" the governor replies, expressionless. The teacher does not react, saying instead, "She's a right little madam, full of 'I beg your pardon's' when she first arrived."

"Bet they soon knocked that out of her," the man says. Like virginity, Lucy's aura of New Person cannot last forever. She arrived there straight from a private school; the Towles miscalculated on a small legacy, and her removal was swift. The new school is near enough for her to walk there.

She clutches the wax crayon. They are doing maps. No colour can go next to itself. Lucy finds it difficult to read the names of the countries, especially all the tiny ones in Eastern Europe. It is easier to mouth them aloud. She is somewhere near the centre on the thoughtful 'circle of achievement' on the wall behind her, meaning she is virtually bottom of the class. IQ is taken into consideration somewhere in the chart, but they have never been able to test Lucy's because she can never see the point of the tests. She always cracks the number codes in the wrong way, or sees patterns that are not there, or assumes the stick men are the same person rather than separate individuals. She is told she does not value other humans sufficiently and is made to work on her interpersonal skills.

The IQ is really a very middle class kind of benchmark but, in an age of classification, journalists, faced by the lifestyles of those they do not understand, write down their subject's score as if it will explain everything. "Josie has 11 rings in her nose and cuts a notch in her leg every time she makes a new friend. She thinks of it as an offering. She keeps tarantulas in a bowl, and feeds them live voles in front of a paying audience. Josie has an IQ of 165."

Lucy is given lots and lots of reading tests, proving again and again that she cannot pronounce 'phythisis', or 'logorrhoea', or even 'ladder' when she has to read them off the page. She keeps handing in pictures with her clumsy, unfinished essays, always of snow. However, despite her teachers' bemused silence at her work, Lucy still smiles with pride. It is suggested that dyslexia is the Devil's work.

"My parents like things to be white. They prefer it," she says, out of ear and eye-shot of the class. She loves the white crayons, the creamy wax varnishing the page, streaked by minute flecks of dirt, like reversed pictures of the stars' movements. But today, "No, Lucy, NO, for crying out loud!"

Lucy has never understood this phrase, for the teacher is crying out loud. Two weeks ago Lucy took some milk from the fridge at home and left the carton sitting in the corner of her room. That morning, she picked up the carton and shook it, the blunt thud showing its progress. It was ready. She took it to school and, after finishing her map, painted a picture with the contents, the smell freshly rank. *The Cheese of Heavenly Fruit of the Cow*, she called it, pleased with the poetry in the name, better than the stuff the teacher implores them to examine and which look to her like ranks of insects moulting on the page. Lucy finds the printed word very difficult to understand.

"Oh Lucy, it stinks!" the teacher hisses as the smell hits the governor.

"She didn't get that here, that's for sure," he murmurs sardonically. "Our stuff never goes off." Lucy smiles.

It has long been a prerequisite of coolness, or at least group acceptability, to turn up late and to have an untidy bedroom. Many tests appear to prove that, in fact, the disordered mind represents a greater clarity of thought. At Lucy's school awards are given to the most insouciant child. At spontaneous intervals, bags are tipped out behind screens and their owners questioned to make sure they do not know exactly what is in them. Class times are only ostensible. In fact they are slated to start 15 to 20 minutes before they really do. Lucy always arrives first and sits, looking straight ahead, until the others come. She always smiles.

At break, her schoolmates mock her blouses. She watches her mother run around before work every day of her life, and that is what she knows. So she asks for a blouse like her mother's. They are really very reasonably priced compared with what the other kids are demanding and getting, and especially next to Steel Hempen.

Steel Hempen is what every child desires. The originals are woven at a discreet, but fashionable, outlet in the East End and then copied by similar, but ersatz, establishments throughout the city. Children want the mystery of a deal, and Steel Hempen's discreet flyers are dropped by the vanful, especially outside primary schools. The address of the main depot is obvious to any child with some knowledge of a certain computer game. When it opened, the trendiest of Lucy's classmates rushed, on their junior travelcards, to an artificially blackened street in the

East End and, if chosen by the balaclavaed assistants, purchased fitted robes in coppery brown or ochre light poly-fibre chainmail. The younger ones in the school, the six and seven year olds, come back with begging stories so pleadingly alarming that their parents can do nothing but hurry down to see. Parents aren't allowed to enter the building on the orders of the adults who run it. They are forced to crane their necks, from a distance, at the living models that strut around in the loud and flickering darkness before silently handing over the appropriate cash through a hatch.

Lucy doesn't want a Steel Hempen, she wants a blouse. She gets several, all white, one with a high neck and little covered buttons and a zip down the back which scratched, a batwing one with tight cuffs and several in the style of a man's shirt, but prettier.

Spring is coming, and the weather, while still cold, tantalises the humans with moments of warm breeze that smell of summer. There are enough of these to allow the children to go outside during break, their hair picked up and tugged by the wind even before they manage to do it to each other. Lucy stands with her back to a tree.

"Lucy new girl! All white! All right!" the children sing, rubbing their hands over the dusty windows and then hugging her tightly.

"I don't think there should be fights," says Lucy. The boy grabs another boy and they run away.

"Ram ram! Ram ram!" they chant.

"I don't like computers," says Lucy.

"What's your mum 'n' dad got?"

"I don't know."

"Holy scrote, Lucy. You fucking fool!"

The wheeling mosaic of TV quotes, mild menaces and impatient reasoning grinds to a soft halt. Steels are appearing. The Steels never run, nor even seem to move fast. Once the clothes are put on, a regality overcomes the wearer. A few of them wear the coveted sandals of which, deliberately, few are released at any one time.

"Leave 'er alone, dolegeeks," says a girl with braided red hair, green eyes and freckled skin the colour of Golden Virginia. The silenced crowd moves away. Lucy knows there's always one who will try to protect her, via the laws of redistribution of power. A truly powerful person should always be seen to be sympathetic, even if they are engaging in torture.

"Lucy piss-queen, what's the pretty shirt for?"

"I like my blouse. My parents bought it for me. I like to wear it." There is a spurt of controlled laughter. The word 'like' has almost fallen out of use among those below a certain age. If something is appreciated, it is 'wanted'. Once obtained, it is 'mine'. Once 'mine' it cannot not be discussed except in terms of what will supercede it soon. Past is rammed into future like a wet fist in a bulb-less socket.

The redhead pulls the blouse out of Lucy's waistband and squeezes her chest around the nipple.

"What do you know about cystitis?"

The world of sticks and bits of string and blocks with words written on them is long gone. What would Arthur Mee think of those little hands now, what they are used for? Those chattering armies of little flower faces, turned upwards at learning, had matured to fruit as hard as pebbles, plucked early from the tree and rolling downhill, not rotting safely in the sweet grass. In the school, the only safe living things are the unprotected saplings around the paved area between the building and the gate. A generation's environmental awareness has elevated plants to the status of gang members. Every sect has a tree around which its members sit at milk break.

The redhead's question sits baldly in the air. Lucy has attended some of the sex education classes offered by the school but, although her health is generally good, she finds herself becoming ill on the mornings they are due to learn about babies, organs, and movements. The sickness only lifts when the classes end. At these times her mother flutters around her particularly attentively. Lucy has not yet evolved far enough to make a connection, although she has been yanking out the hairs that newly persist in growing on her. She's missed the 'diseases' class, the penultimate one before they did 'love'. Lucy is not sure why she was ill the morning they did *that* class, but suddenly on the Monday she was unable to open her eyes, and her whole body felt heavy. She does not know how to answer the girl's question, but tries anyway.

"Have they got a new record out?" The Steels hiss with laughter, on and on and on.

"Should take her down the Wolf brothers. They'd sort her out!"

"Yeah! My brother says he saw Pete Wolf once, outside 'arrods, tryin' to snort this 'ole pile of snow."

"What, real snow?"

"Yeah, 'e says 'e could do mind over matter stuff! Like one-a them phakkirs—"

"Phakkirs – *Moral!* Now their new album's *able!* Try that one, Lucywhite."

"Oldonaminit, wot's your bruv doin' outside Harrods then?"

There is a click of snapped fingers as the chief girl expresses her boredom with the way the conversation is going.

"Tits coming, Lucywhite." The Steel girls in this school have already demanded an extra double lesson on sexuality. In class they sit together in pairs, hands holding each others' thighs, utterly attentive to the teacher. They laugh at Lucy, and push her. So everyone copies them.

But somehow it is all token. No-one is truly frightening, particularly after milk break. Then, when mellow silence comes over the school for a while, bored, Lucy goes to her coat and finds bars of chocolate in it. She is still not sure why everyone apart from her loses interest in everything at 10.45 in the morning, nor who is putting things in her pockets. Once she found a floppy disc, which she took and put into one of the school computers. The whole system crashed instantly, images of magma streaming down the screens, and every machine had to be cleaned up by a team of engineers working around the clock for two days. She apologised, claiming ignorance of the virus scanner, saying there is no machine at home. *White* lies, she had always heard at home, are quite acceptable. A teacher took her aside and asked her if everything was OK with mum and dad/carer/guardian.

Lucy stands with her back against a tree, facing the giggling crowd. A narrow figure appears in the school doorway, wrapped in a grey shawl. It makes its way uncertainly towards the little group, its lips moving silently as if counting to ten. It stops about six feet from them and speaks weakly, its thumbnail in its mouth.

"No ceremonies. Stop it now, you girls." This is a woman whose shouting once temporarily deafened a child in one ear. Not realising it had lost the use of the ear, the child turned up the volume of its Walkman, and then collapsed, blood pouring from its head. Thankfully, things were ironed out with swift and public discipline which appeased the parents; the child became eligible for an index linked grant, payable by the school, partly from the teacher's wages. The woman was not sacked, however, as people of her calibre were in short supply. Recently, there have been a couple of sudden absences amongst the female staff, so she is needed more than ever.

Today the teacher seems to have shrunk, in both sound and physical volume. She seems to be walking around in an increasingly dense cloud of interference. And she is sweating. The Steels ignore her and continue to stare at Lucy. Finally the teacher comes near enough to peer down over their heads.

"Come on now, go and get your milk."

The chief Steal, hardly looking at her, all slang gone, says, "She's not feeling very confident is she? Bet she wishes she got up to what we did last night. But she can't, because she's too repressed!"

"What's it like, Adele, watching from the sidelines while kids get the kicks you're too weak to investigate?" chimes in another.

They are quoting from *Teach Me and Die,* a cartoon sitcom about a family of educationalists. Their mimicry is perfect.

"Let's wait for her to tell us what she got up to last night, with her bowl of tuna splat and *single* portion of apple compote!" They all fold their arms and looked at her. The teacher has been told never to wring her hands. She stands over them, like a young giraffe that has accidentally come upon a group of hungry, mutant hyenas. Lucy sees a tear rising in one of her eyes.

"But I want a lacto, soonest," murmurs another girl.

"We stare," says the boss. To encourage the others, she adds, "Bet Adele's never injected sulphate into her thigh!"

"My mum used to!" chimes someone, half-heartedly. No-one says anything else. Time passes.

"I wanna lacto, I'm dying," asserts another girl, scratching her own face deeply.

"We stare." The teacher is trembling. She can barely look at Lucy, her little chin like a cut-out over the high, tight neck of her blouse. After a while, there is dissent among these young skins. Fingers rub eyes, running noses and ears; breaths come faster. Someone pulls out a nutmeg grater, obviously stolen, and begins scraping it up and down her arms.

"No more stare. Lacto! White juice!"

"Come on, it's not worth it! Let's hit the crate." There is a rising sense of alarm, as heads begin shaking involuntarily from side to side. Even the boss's knuckles are whitening as she tries not to shake. The teacher stands her ground. Loyalty evaporates.

"NOW." One girl, scratching rapidly, turns and scuttles indoors. Others follow. The leader, now unable to ride out her withdrawal, turns and walks off, with an attempt at dignity as she trembles. Lucy expects the teacher to approach her and touch her shoulder, tell her that bullies are cowards, and ask again if everything is OK with the parental rolers. But she does not. If anything, she looks more afraid.

"Milk time, Lucy."

"Oh, it's all right, I don't want any."

"Milk time!" the teacher spits, her fists clenched. Lucy walks slowly back into the building, where the Steels are sitting around. They smile at her.

After school, Lucy walks alone out of the gate. Streaming cries of "Lorkthamerthie Mithter Thnipe!" a crude imitation of the shady, lisping second-hand software dealer in *2-Bit Outfit,* a wildly popular cartoon series, carry her home.

Reg has hired a sledgehammer. She goes into the back bedroom and knocks down the dividing wall between the spare bedroom and the room next to it, where she hangs spare costumes. She is soon covered in plaster and partition dust, like a sadhu rubbed in ash before he presses his face into the Ganges. She finishes the fiddly bits with a shoe, its stiletto heel soon stripped of its leather, the metal exposed like bone. Her Ganges is coming.

Her possessions, as she throws them, seem fragile, trivial compared with the warm smooth metal and intricate technology she is going to replace them with. Deliveries come: a crate of mice; a microscope with a copious selection of hypodermic needles, some finer than the eye can see, and piles of different shaped small glass dishes.

Night comes, and the wall is nearly done. The hole is big and still round. From way down in her Reg feels a girder of emotion ram upwards through her heart and out between her eyes. She begins to cry uncontrollably. It is a long time since she has done anything like that. There is a ring at the doorbell. "Special Delivery Madam." Without thinking, she lets them in. Then she forgets she has done that and starts sweeping the floor; her face is a hole as the flood opens. There is a sound at her door.

"SURPRISE!" There is a yell, and someone comes high kicking through the door holding a splashing petrol can. It is Danny. He takes a huge gulp of petrol and roars, before diving over the floor and skidding to a halt at Regina's feet, which he starts to bite.

"Happy Valentine's day, you old cow!" Miraculously, the petrol can has not fallen over, and he indicates it. It is full of home-made wine.

"Regina I love you! Don't cry!"

He climbs onto her and pushes his face up her skirt and clamps his lips against her flesh. Simultaneously, he begins to sing against her. It is like a kazoo and Reg is soon crying out with laughter and craving to be fucked. He does not do this, but forces her to come and come, like bullets underwater.

"Reg, what the fuck are you doing?" he shouts as he raises his head and sees the room.

It takes about a week to transform the new space. While she works, it never once crosses Reg's mind that she might be indulging in nostalgia, dredging up and worshipping graven images of loss. The mice seem banal, reminding her of school, but they are a start. She would rather use swans, bears or monkeys, the animals she most hates, this sinister trinity of semi-heraldic beasts, drenched in sentimental symbolism that fails to mask the stench beneath. Exalted by her fantasies, she orders some rats.

Time passes, and Regina waters her plants, picking and twirling with needles at stamens and roots. Thinking she is not a torturer, she tries to mix a tiger lily with a mouse, gently rubbing the flaming dust on its rear.

A new force is born when two sets of genes collide, so the whole ought to be greater than the sum of its ancestors. But many of the thousands of people Regina has met in her life are clearly not so. They are the inevitable product of cells joining when there is no love.

Reg needs her creatures, reject as well as perfect, to prove things to herself. Her beauty and aura gain her entry to certain laboratories and farms, most of whom are intensely shy of revealing the offcuts and misfires from their breeding programmes. However, when she offers the management her services for free they soon relent.

Then she begins to search for co-thinkers. She spends Christmas Day posting and posting until the first pulses of the seemingly like-minded come back to her. A short ad on a popular science website, headed, *Are you Dominant or Recessive? Come and show me!* throws up a teenage public schoolboy, angelic and blubber-lipped. In a shed at the bottom of his parents' garden, he tinkers with goldfish and hamsters won at fairs. He calls himself a neo-eugenicist. One frosty evening, the street lights hidden behind houses, the boy takes Reg to the shed and makes her peer through the sharp-scented gloom at the blobs of awkward flesh quivering on soaked cotton wool.

"They're just lives," he says, at Reg's frown.

"Their souls deserve better," she responds. Later, Reg slips into the garden from the back and suffocates them. Pictures of warfare slip into her mind, of Hiroshima, remaindered humans. As she kills them she notices the boy's unusually large collection of long-banned 1950s army watches, their luminous faces burning. Enough of them, even given the half-life, to mash the genes of these creatures.

She sees no correlation between the preparations for her show and this boy's tinkering sadism. Her one-eyed mice will do very well. The nearer the centre the eye grows, the more ruthlessly she will destroy the rest. "It's impossible to look into someone's eyes – try it!" she once hissed at a departing lover. You cannot truly look into both of a person's eyes at once without constant movement; there is no stillness in love. Her next urge is to breed her little creatures with their hearts on their front legs, beating there for all to see.

It's getting dark. Lucy walks down street after street. She really should be accompanied in this day and age. There is a bang against the wall behind her, and the noise of crumbs of brickwork falling. Feet sound from down the other end of the road. Lucy turns and sees figures running towards her. She runs too. As she turns a corner a window pane explodes just above her head. There are shouts. The people behind her turn and disappear. Lucy runs home without looking back.

"Lorksamerthie!" Lucy cackles idly as she trips through the door of her home. The front door bangs. In the Towle's front hallway sits a gate in the form of a wagon wheel that you have to push past in order to get in, as if to census everyone who lives there or visits. On the wall is a display of vicious-looking antique African combs. The walls are bistre beige with a hint of oatmeal. In this house, nothing is left to chance. Even the chairs have stabilisers on them. Lucy is not often allowed to use a knife. Mr Towle cuts up her food for her into regular cubes.

Lucy goes into the toilet. The radio is shouting from the kitchen.

When Lucy finally enters the living room, her father is joggling her mother on his knee while she idles through some yellowing transparencies. Boxes of varying shapes and sizes are delivered to the flat on a regular basis, always wrapped in brown paper, and swiftly pulled into a locked cupboard by Mr Towle. One has clearly arrived today. Mrs Towle is flushed, her hair sticking up.

"Lorksamerthie! Gorda disease in me config-SYS, sister! Sorw-id" Lucy misquotes madly and tears up the inner stairs to her room.

"Lucy! What did you say?" The warmth emanating from the living room pools and swishes up the chimney. There is a familiar, cultured silence, broken only by the dog hammering at the inside of a cupboard. Mugs swing on their hooks.

"What did you say?"

"I says the cat is stupid."

"We don't have a cat any more, Lucy, as you know. We have a dog. Do you not know the difference?" As Lucy comes to the door, her mother's voice is iron under frayed velvet.

"We don't like you using those words, they're so old-fashioned. You're not a little cockney, darling, are you? I know you're our little tin lid, but I think we're trying to take things a little far, aren't we? And can't you think of anything new to say? The word, if you must use it, is 'sorted', not 'sorw–id'."

"She isn't, very," murmurs her father.

"So every time you use them, we dock your kiddy tax. Now, repeat after me, 'sorted'."

"A stitch in time saves nine," singsongs her father, peering up her mother's skirt as she rises over Lucy. Lucy looks at the carpet.

"Just look at her, our little working miss!"

"I'm not little," says Lucy.

"Don't answer back."

"She does quack on." Lucy is silent.

"Lucy, you're scared. Don't be so wet! Oh look at her – when she's bigger she'll be able to wear my clothes and save us one heck of a lot of money." Mr Towle pulls timidly at Mrs Towle's hem, looking up at her.

"Cuissade, cuissade," he murmurs urgently, as if asking to be sat on the pot. But Mrs Towle hasn't finished with her daughter.

"Look at all your friends, well, if you have any. Give us something to row about, please. We're waiting with much trepidation for your teenage rebellion, Lucy."

"If her current behaviour is anything to go by, I doubt it'll be up to much,' Mr Towle presses his nose against his wife's behind and sniffs.

"Why've I been ill all-time when sex classes is on?"

" 'ARE', not 'IS', 'ARE' on, not 'IS' on." her parents roar in unison. Lucy goes up to her room.

At one and a half Lucy was put into harness to straighten her back because a grandfather had developed a premature hump. At three she was given wrist weights to make her strong because the mother feared she would grow up thin armed like several members of her husband's family. At five her mother started to encourage, then enforce, master-servant games. Lucy learnt to save all her energy for running from Ride of the Valkyrie.

Below, Reg feels something emanating. Weakly perhaps, as it has to come through two ceilings, but there is definitely a faint and husky cry seeping down at her from someone. That night, Reg dreams that every vein and artery in her body is rippling up and rising into a dense cat's cradle in the air. Simultaneously, Lucy dreams she is a new-born tadpole, plunging in a sea of eggs and spawn, jelly nubs of life, splashing in tiny growths, inhaling them. And then a net plunges into the water and scoops her up. The front door bangs again downstairs.

"Granny let's go to the beach!
And your stick will bloom like a tree-ee-ee
And in each wrinkle-furrow grows new life, new life!
Granny! Grann-eee!"

Lucy sings the ballad as Old Mrs Towle comes up the stairs the next morning. There is not an ounce of flesh on Old Mrs Towle, who is really New Mrs Towle, with the accrual of her deceased husband's life insurance. Any spare has long been cut away and invisible scars left in its place. There is nothing left to stretch, so she eats carefully. 'Granny' is not a word she ever uses herself, but she indulges Lucy with a wave of her flashing hand.

"What a prescient little person! That's exactly where we're all going for the weekend. I'll drive!" Old Mrs Towle leads the family down the stairs. Regina, stiff from the previous night's dreaming, leans against the wall to let them pass. Her lips hang out like hulls, creamed over with a soft purplish red that plasters the dry cracks in them. And nobody had even been round last night. Old Mrs Towle feels Reg's look on her like a fine spray of glycerine that takes her persona and dissolves it. Reg doesn't say a word. She stoops, her shoulder blades like wings discreetly furled and straining her clothing, and looks over the family group as they pass her, trying, while only moving her eyes, to catch Lucy's. Lucy is encased in hair, coat and gloves. Reg holds the security door open for them as they pass down to the next floor. No-one says a word. This is the first time Reg has seen them in close-up since they moved in, although they appear to have seen her. For the first time in her life Reg actually feels the 'bad vibes' she is always warning her clients about. She winces with dislike for them, apart from the little girl, who arouses a strange feeling in her.

The Towles drive to Lyme Regis, Lucy and her mother in the back. Lucy stares out of the window as modest suburb follows modest suburb, country flashing a little between each. Gradually true countryside begins to appear, after the little houses, traffic lights and contraflows. New Mrs Towle drives with her jewellery on, bracelets and rings and earrings clunking with each movement. She loves the display, which is why she has never got an automatic. Mr Towle talks about the weather, and Mrs Towle hisses at him and glares at his mother from behind. The car smells new. There is nothing on the floor behind the seats for Lucy to fiddle with. Her grandmother hands her a fresh pack of cards. Lucy shuffles them for the next four hours until they are warm and damp and browned. They arrive at the underground car park, the car rocking over the humps, and stand around the vehicle, already at a loose end. The cold air seems to tear at Lucy after the car's fuggy sac.

"Awful place, darlings, mind the Hovis Pullovis as you go!" New Mrs T points to a straggle of anoraked tourists looking for their coach. Silence falls on the Towles as they leave the building. They well know that with each new set of car park muggings comes a more vicious security firm, who in turn began looting cars themselves, and so are replaced by another company whose employees themselves soon fall tempted to attack and brutalise. This time, however, the Towles are lucky and arrive outside without incident. Smelling sea air, Lucy jumps up and down.

"The sea! The sea! Let's go down now."

"It's winter darling, we can't swim today," says her grandmother.

"I don't wanna swim. I want the water and the air and the fish!"

" 'Want to', not 'wanna'," says Mrs Towle. They walk slowly around a museum whose exhibits are either high up in glass cases or enormous lumps of reproduction war machinery painted black. Then they go to a restaurant papered with deep green plush.

During soup, Lucy shreds her napkin. During main course, she taps her fork along her teeth and plays with the pain on her filling. During pudding, she etches faces in the top of a crème brûlée. No-one says anything to her about anything. During coffee, she says, "What does copulate mean?" Her mother instantly, yet with care, pulls a holly stalk from the table display and jams it against her hand, with the words, "Look at the pretty berries on this plant!"

"My darling," says her grandmother earnestly, "whatever are they teaching you in school? Good gracious, Simon's two could probably get themselves a thriving gynie practice tomorrow and they can barely reach the door handle, except that I think Robert's gay. Yes, yes I definitely think he's gay, no two ways about it, and you can't really in all honesty have a homosexual gynaecologist, not really." Her voice trails off, pleasantly. The candles die in their glasses.

It is getting dark by the time they leave. Lucy hears no waves. It is still and cold, the traffic is loud and the water does not have the energy to show white. They walk along the front as the lights go on. Suddenly there is a soft musical cry from half-way down the Cobb. They walk nearer, Mr Towle a little nervous. A dark-skinned woman, dressed in period costume, is singing while playing a guitar. It needs wind, that sound. The stone of the Cobb takes its share of the noise and flattens it in the dusk. The notes are operatic but intimate. There is no point in throwing money. It will be lost. Lucy throws a shiny bottle cap she finds on the ground. She has to give something. The sound of its fall distracts the singer for a moment.

"Lucy, don't be so rude."

"I wasn't."

"Don't contradict." The singer is finishing her shift, as she always does, where money cannot be raised. Foolish perhaps. She sings on. For a few moments no traffic passes and the sound is seamless.

"That woman's amazing," whispers Lucy.

"When will you stop glamorising black people? And why is she wearing that silly outfit. Is she protesting?" murmurs her father.

"It's a free country, innit?" says Lucy, the words imprinted on her mind from somewhere as a suitable response to adult assertions.

"Lucy! How many times do I have to tell you not to say that. This is not a 'free country', as you please to call it, and thank God for that! That bloody witchy woman downstairs, you think she's God's gift just because she's a bit darker skinned than we are. It's quite extraordinary. She looks like a gyppo to me."

" 'Isn't it', not 'innit'. She does witter on, doesn't she?" says Mrs Towle. "I can't believe this little thing is ours. How I wish we had a boy, a tall dark curly-haired boy who could play rugby and the violin."

"And spell the English Language."

"It must be bad genes."

"Yours, then."

"I can't see myself in her, to be honest."

"Well you spewed her out ten and a half years ago."

"Ugh, don't remind me. Anyway, she looks like you, so you can take the main responsibility for her uselessness."

Mr Towle produces a look of triumph. "Perhaps we adopted you, Lucy, what do you think of that?" Mrs Towle, suddenly, turns on him. "Alan! How could you be so horrible to our lovely little Lucy!" Her voice becomes a complicitous whisper. "Oh Lucy, I'm the only one who knows how wonderful you are. He only sees what other people see."

The little group turns and walked briskly back towards the streets. The woman winds up her singing and follows them at a distance. She wants to take the little girl back to her flat, give her a bowl of pasta and a lager, and lace it with a drug so powerful that she will only wake up when she is big enough to leave home. The little group spends an hour and a half in the bar of their hotel, Lucy hushed every time her voice rises above a slight murmur. She is small enough to get away with wandering round empty tables and popping crisp packets. Boredom overcomes her like a shroud as she picks crumbs of beef & onion from her hair.

The next day, they drive and visit an old tower. It has coloured signs all over it, and a shop. They walk in a tour group to the top of it. There is nothing to see on the windy battlements but dull green fields.

Lucy follows the tour group to the plaqued entrance of the tower and follows slowly up the fine worn spiral staircase after them.

"Is your little girl all right?" asks a man.

"My little daughter thinks she is retreating into a very adult depression," said Mr Towle. "She's a silly little child pretending to be an adult. Children don't have feelings like that. She's just in a sulk, that's all."

Lucy's fury is a tidal wave inside her. The tour guide leads the group around the tiny battlements to look at the view. Lucy stays where she is.

Lucy, the wind raping her dry eyes, walks slowly to the edge of the ancient stairway and pitches herself down the steps. Each step is cupped smooth with years of feet. The spiral traps her, the white light, useless through the arrow slits, flashing into her eyes. Lucy has no last thought as she throws herself down into the dark air. She thinks she will easily come to rest on one of the wide edges of the steps but she keeps on going, spinning like a crab, tumbling close to the tiny useless strips of stone that radiate from the central cylinder. Above, the voices are silent as the tourists appreciate the fine view. Lucy soils their silence with the screech of her anorak against the stone, the clap of her little three-buckled shoes turning over and over, faster and faster, her hair yanking from every pore as her body traps and untraps it. Lucy stops falling when she reaches the feet of the next tour group as the guide prepares to shout up the stairs in the traditional way. Lucy looks up at him and smiles, her face chalky from the scraping. The wind up here has dried her skin.

"Little girl, what are you doing?" The man projects his voice up the stairway, maybe hoping for a laugh from amongst his charges. One of her arms is broken, a rib cracked, one ankle suspected broken. Lucy feels great joy as she lies out of the whining winds. She hears her mother's shoes clapping on the steps and the chorused "oh-oh" of the women behind her.

"Lucy, Lucy!" she cries, and under the echo of the cry, through clenched teeth, "what the hell have you done now? Are you deliberately trying to spoil our holiday?" Lucy, beached below her, is loving every second of it. The little crowds mingle and flutter at the shining little girl with the arm bent like a hairpin, foot lying uselessly to the side. The ambulance throws up dust from the car park, spraying the dawdling tourists and perking them up for an instant. Lucy smiles on, blood crusting from a graze above her eyebrow, labia bruised with impact as she spun clumsily down the stairs.

The hospital is dated and worn.

"We're going to give you a little prick now Lucy, to take away the pain."

"That's what Daddy is, aren't you, Daddy! That's what mum says!" The nurse advances.

"It's OK, I don't need it, really I don't!" The nurse gets really close. Close enough to see the hardness in Lucy's eyes. Without warning, Lucy sticks her hand out, palm flat, straight onto the needle. Its tip peeps out between the pores on her hand. Her skin is seeped over with black and blue ink like henna. Lucy sometimes holds a biro and cuts symbols into herself as she walks so that her hand is washed with a tide of pale wedgewood under the hot royal navy of fresh ink. The nurse shudders with horror, waiting on the lawsuit that will surely follow. But this little girl's father seems more concerned with family politics than litigation, for which she can only be grateful.

"You see what she did!" The nurse murmurs self-righteously, trying to extricate the needle. "We should be using guns by now!" she adds petulantly. In this old place the visibly disposable has died hard. Lucy laughs brightly in the irritable silence. The nurse, seeing the law is not about to be called upon, relaxes. Since some of her female colleagues have been off sick recently, she has negotiated a handsome raise in salary, and a new job-title, for replacing some of them. The doctor decides to try the old cartoon trick of pinching Lucy to distract her from the pain. Lucy laughs delightedly, sits up and leans forward on her twisted ankle.

"I don't need it, really I don't!" Lucy's bliss at the shriek of misplaced bone on bone is utter.

Lucy takes the pills simply to escape a verbal cauterisation by her parents. She lies back and floats. She presses at her chest to find the pain and pushes at the injured beams of herself.

Pain killers render her weak, making her stare up at the ceiling, a blob of life, a cramped little bud. When they wear off, and the sound of torn nerve and hysterical synapse again becomes audible, she rises up from her bed with joy. She learns to hold the pills in her mouth and spit them into her hand.

Lucy dreams that skeins of herself are being sucked out through her mouth, vagina and anus, but there is no blood, no warm cascade of life juice, just human wire. A voice calls to her with love and encouragement.

In her next dream Lucy sits, soaked, in a pen while fat pigs, gorged on blood, lie on their sides, their flesh taking root in the ground as they die. Lucy plays with their ears and tails, tiny in an infinite red-stained field.

The car smells cloying on the way home.

A sunny morning. Reg is throwing up. Acid chunks of fibrous red mulch stick in her hair, which is growing fast in spite of the cold. As she kneels on the tiles a dog runs in again with the peculiar little howdah on its back, as if a doll could ride there. This is phase two, Reg trying to grow grass on the dog's skin, on a poultice of peat and bone mash adapted from cattle feed. It is meant to breach the gap between moving flesh and anchored root; the richer, more human mixture near the living hide. She hopes the plant will be driven to speed up and take root in the dog, who does not seem to mind. The experiment has to be boxed in with half a pair of diving goggles, so the dog does not scratch itself. She heaves again and misses the toilet bowl, distracted by the dog. It laps gratefully at the red froth on the ground. As she works, Reg feels a serenity she has never felt before, a smooth satisfaction with her days, as if she is preparing.

Reg gives the ointment to her first clients of the day, recommending minute amounts this time, warning them that they may also throw up and start behaving strangely, hinting also that she is intending to wind down her business.

Later she goes out. There are police in the street, and a small cordon. The air is sharp. There is a slight mist. She waits for the bus. The first one she sits on breaks down, windows jammed open, in front of a house in a quiet street. She sits and looks down into the nearest garden.

Two children are playing there. A little girl in red walks over to where her brother is standing holding a basket of foil-covered eggs. While the boy is distracted, she takes one from the basket and carries it back to the magnolia bush where she has put her own basket. And so on back and forth. The little boy is transfixed by the squirrels. As the little girl removes an egg, she replaces each one with a stone so that he won't notice the basket getting lighter. Twelve eggs later, there are 12 rough, dusty iron-stone pebbles flaking together in the wicker. The squirrels suddenly run off, snaking through the dewy grass up into a tree. The little boy looks down at his eggs and instead of purple and gold foil sees cold rocks.

He looks up and sees the little girl, now as absorbed with the eggs as he was with the squirrels, sitting with her basket between her knees in the sunlight. Mother is coming from the kitchen to call them for breakfast and – wait a minute, that's the nice woman Reg treated earlier in the day – the little boy is accelerating towards the little girl, doubt still buzzing around his head about where his eggs are. Then he sees the flash of gold through the magnolia and runs redoubtably towards the little girl, still gripping the basket. Even he doesn't know what he is going to do with the basket when he gets over to the little girl. Now, the mother is on her way out of the house. All this takes very little time as the garden is small.

And as the little boy runs and runs toward the little girl, she raises her basket high and screams, "Mummy, mummy, look what I've got!" With her basket on her arm she jumps up to run towards her mother at the same time as the little boy reaches top speed and brings his basket down upon her head. But there is no head. She is gone. The boy overbalances with the lack of the little girl beneath him and falls to the ground.

Just then, as a ray of sun falls on the kitchen window, the mother stops moving and stands, rigid and transfixed at the sight of her children, hands clasping her face. She lets out a soundless scream and disappears. Reg can just hear heels on kitchen lino, the frenzied dragging of a bag over ranged crockery, the sound of smashing, and then feet again, out of the door and down the street. Reg is about to run off the bus after her when suddenly it grinds into life and moves away. The children look at where their mother has gone.

Her mobile purrs. It is Lou. Reg is momentarily cowed by the voice at the other end of the phone.

"Reggie! I've been taking some of my old jewellery round the markets but no-one wants it. They keep wittering something about old jewellery having spirits in it which might get passed on. I mean, it's so silly. You would have thought they'd have seen my plight and allowed me my prosperity!"

Reg feels a twinge of guilt, since it's her who has largely contributed to the idea's prevalence in the first place. She persuaded anyone wearing old jewellery that they should not be wearing it for fear of bad vibes, and offered to cleanse it for them. Having amassed a small pile, she sold it all and told them she had been burgled.

Lou sounds knackered. Reg prays Lou's baby will turn to radiant ether and disappear before it can be born.

"I want you to be there for me when he comes out!" breathes Lou. "I'm calling him Benjamin!"

"Oh, I didn't know you'd checked," says Reg idly, the sight of the fleeing woman burning in her eyes.

"Silly, I know what I'm talking about!"

"OK, OK," Reg murmurs.

"Now Reggie, the reason I'm calling is that I'd like you to meet my friends, the people I've met through Johnny. They're all wonderful, sincere human beings. We're having one of our dinners next week. You will come, won't you?"

When Reg gets back later, a reporter is chafing at doors in her road, asking about a bullet that was found.

"Bog off!" Reg's hair feels thick. She calls Phil and Jamie. She'll get more of the drug and sell it on to someone else.

"Jamie, hi it's Reg."

"Regina! Hi." He sounds a bit too efficient. Trying too hard.

"Got any more of that stuff."

"Maybe. Yes. Is the stuff working? No problems?"

"Problems! It's brought me loads of new business! Too much almost. All the women seem to be getting the same effects."

"Chill-out yeah? Top of the world, yeah?" His voice lifts.

"Funny you should say that, Jamie. By some weird coincidence, they've all discovered that they hate children. Silly isn't it. Must be a political drug! I'm sure it won't do them any harm though. Oh I just thought, it can't be them who're going round shooting kids, can it? That must be one of those misogynist myths the press like throwing at us. I'm sick of it all, frankly. Fucking media! Always two years behind!"

There is a silence at the end of the line.

four

LUCY LIES AGAINST THE TOILET WALL, smiling, her arm in a sling. She has just been beaten up and had the mother-of-pearl buttons ripped from her blouse. She lies like a slag, someone says, clothes ripped open, legs apart, head thrown forward, hair in her mouth. She spirals her finger in the water that pools on the uneven buttermilk-coloured tiles. She thinks for a moment that she has become another lavatory. It is only logical. She is sitting at right angles to the one already there, back straight, knees splayed and bent, all upturned for other's use.

"You're not a child," her mother wrote to her on the Mininet this morning, "you are some sort of vegetable, an animated vegetable, or vegetablised animal. I can peel you and peel you and it all grows back the same. It's so strange that you don't change." The words glow over the Mininet. The previous evening, her father tried to teach her to spell. She could not. He shouted at her and ended by hitting her, lightly but sharply, his voice sounding as it always does, as if he is reacting to something else going on behind her.

"Other children your age can spell, why can't you? Disappointment has moved into this house on a permanent basis. I'm thinking of charging it rent! In fact, yes, that's it! It can stay in your room and you can sleep downstairs on the sofa. Bloody hell! The milk's like a brick! The butter's turned grey! What is this? Are there freak storms over Tokyo or what? The smell! I think the fridge is playing up. Lucy! Have you done something to our fridge in some sort of teeny weeny little insurrection?"

Lucy was sent to her room. Mrs Towle has been drinking more, has scuff marks on her hands and occasionally coughs blood. Mr Towle is developing shingles. Both, however, are proud of their ostensibly blame-free histories, steeped in timid rectitude. For them, the getting of medical help will not be such a problem.

Now, Lucy can count herself lucky as she sits on the toilet floor, a voice from somewhere inside her speaking words of love to her. Things could be worse. Lucy could be a girl she knows from school called Feef, whose parents are out of work coppers. They offer Feef cigarettes before sitting her down under a lamp to ask her where she's been. Feef has bruises. Lucy does not, not really. And Feef wears low cut tops over her flat chest, and cannot hide the marks except with a nylon scarf. Lucy wears high necks, which hide quite a lot of things. But she cannot hide her soul.

The other children's violence reaches a peak just before break-time when the milk is handed out, but recently it's tasted strange. Lucy hears a teacher remark that the little ones are becoming harder to control. Another says something about increased immunity, and crosses herself. Regina walked past the school several times in the past week. Lucy waved to her from the playground. Dibby Grant says Reg had picked up his knife for him when he'd thrown it at Steve Miles, missed, and it had gone over the wall, hitting Reg's cheek. She had just wiped it on her scarf and given it back. That was ever so nice of her, most biguns woulda eared him off to the chief cunt.

"I am a toilet," Lucy says to a stray teacher when he tells her off for looking messy.

"I've *been* to the toilet," he corrects; never sure whose first language is English, he always gives the children the benefit of the doubt. He is not really a teacher but a bakery assistant who took a part-time job controlling classes and occasionally correcting the facts offered by the other teachers who have English degrees but little else. He does sex classes as well.

"No, I am a toilet." Lucy observes again. He wishes he was still dodging the bun-stamp at Forsons.

"Radical haddock lobster," he says, figure of eighting his finger around her face. She looks at him solemnly. He shakes his head and leads her back to her class. Rows of children sit with their heads down, drawing, scribbling and thinking. Sex is his favourite subject to teach, because no-one ever interrupts, fights or coughs during it. Lucy has never been to this class before mainly because she was off sick at home, but today's is a last minute rescheduling.

"Herpes, some say, resembles LSD in that it opens new neural pathways from the spine to the vulva. A subsequent sexual act will bring it all back again like a flashback, so it is essential that an attack is neutralised far enough in advance. The fact that there is still no absolute cure indicates the complex power of the neural structures within the body. Claire, do you want to say something?"

"So, if it's like acid, then the pain of a herpes attack must be like a hallucination, an imaginary trip via the dermis and epidermis, leading the sufferer to imagine that they are suffering an external injury, whereas in fact it is an erroneous and violent message engendered entirely inside the body." There is serious nodding in the back row. Someone has dropped a weapon but does not even bother to pick it up.

"Thankyou, Claire, that's very interesting." Lucy thinks her mother's got that, at least she's heard her cursing and screaming, and wailing to Mr Towle that a friend of hers had to be kept in overnight on pethidine because of the pain. And there is silence from Mr Towle who has been unfaithful to his wife, but only by mouth.

"The cold sore and genital sore are largely the same virus so, yes, you can pass it around, back and forth, and kissing is just as bad as sexual intercourse."

Lucy speaks.

"My mum says my dad's got a silly insignificant little prick. Did he give her herpes 'cos of that?" There is a general sneer.

"Ner, ner, Lucywhiteblouse! We did size three months ago. It only matters if you think it does," shouts one boy.

"We think it does!" return some of the girls.

"That's really mean!" another girl shouts at them. "You can't help what you're born with."

"I was a Caesarean, I was born with a knife and rubber gloves!" shouts the boy. Lucy has disrupted the class. It ends and the teacher leaves the room.

"Lucy come here!"

Lucy responds to Francestina Skeggs's call. She is the hardest, and cutest, in her class. She puts her arm around Lucy.

"I'd like you to be my best friend this week, Lucywhite!"

"I'd like you to be my best friend this week," says Lucy. Whoever communicates with her she becomes. Lucy knows it is safer to imitate her closest environment, like the moth or chameleon. They've just done chameleons in Biology. Francestina looks at her. She fosters an atmosphere of entitlement around herself, doling out emotional and material rewards like a professional.

"Someone said your pictures smelt funny later on."

"Someone said your pictures—" Lucy is cut short by a kick in the mouth. But only for a minute. She'd forgotten Francestina is from a kung fu family. Francestina wouldn't have had a chance *not* to learn it. Lucy stares and stares, watching Francestina wait for the expected fear reaction.

"Your hair's going to fall out soon," Lucy whispers, "and you're going to get the worst acne of anyone in this borough."

That night Lucy dreams of the toilet again, but this time she is the seat, curled round, cold but then warmed by others at regular intervals. She feels happy in the dream, for the toilet is connected by pipes and conduits to other toilets, other lives, and thereby to a body of water that is connected to other, larger bodies of water. She is anchored, safe.

She wakes early and does some painting before school, with her fingers and her hair. As a gesture, her mother decides to walk with her that morning. She grabs Lucy's hood as they descend the stairs and jerks it up and down.

"Trot on! Trot on! You know, a Spanish riding school for little girls, now that would be lovely!" She chucks Lucy under the knee with her umbrella.

"Now then, lift your knee, lift it higher, higher, prouder as you walk, what a fine little filly. God your hair smells. We must wash it later." Lucy grips the pictures in her bag.

Electronic billboards grimace and chatter above them. Lucy watches a white balloon and its string fly up against the blip-eyes and slit mouth of the 'before' character in an advert for a new anti-depressant. For a moment it is as if the balloon is a sperm, nudging at the mouth and then upwards and over one eye, perhaps held there by some odd friction. Any hole will do now. Other balloons waft along the street in dull currents. Lucy knows a little bit about sperm from a picture, but does not really understand what they do. She imagines gigantic sperm are coming at her through her tear ducts, that she is the sad man talking on the videoboard above her. The balloon is coming into her eye, and will work its way into her like an elephant down a rabbit hole, inching its way into her body, the membrane will stretch and stretch, her eyeball will be pushed and pushed, the balloon, filled full of thought and personality, its skin as thick as leather, will heave into her eye and back into her head, where the agony will make her insane…

"Lucysilly, stop staring up there, you look like common little tyke with your mouth open, catching flies."

"I've got a balloon in my eye. It's pushing my brain and then it's going to burst and stuff's going to come out of it and make me into God," says Lucy, quietly.

"Vigil-Aunties where are you when I need you?" her mother may or may not have whispered just then, thinking of the raisiny woman who collared her by the bins. "Stop screaming and don't be silly," says Mrs Towle.

The sky lurches again, inexorably. Lucy looks up at her mother and thinks she sees herself. So she begins to copy her every move, walk and word until Mrs Towle slaps her. Mrs Towle looks down at Lucy, and sees there her own pathetic image, or that of her husband's. As she looks irritably up at the videoboard, a vast pigeon dropping plummets out of the sky. Lucy walks on in silence.

Mrs Towle was out again last night.

Reg is itching. She's just taken a call from some students who wanted to "animate some more babies with her", and now some geezer has just rung her doorbell as a "follow-up call" to some junk mail that somehow found its way past all the usual blocks. They ask her if she has anything "more than a hundred years old" to get rid of. They talked in money with a lot of zeros on it. Reg has nothing like that – pre-pre-pre-owned possessions with filthy patinas, the shit of years. They were obviously lying, anyway. If someone has to come to your door to buy or sell you can guarantee it's a dodgy deal. To Reg, antiques stink of a mismanaged spirit world, of exclusion, of trapped thoughts that their previous owners had when they were near them. If she lifts the teeming flagstone of her persona and looks into her heart she knows that what she really wants to do is to smash the toughened glass in every one of those arse-wipe emporia and hand out the stuff from a lorry to every housing estate in the country. She sees herself magnanimously passing an early nineteenth century occasional table, with skinny legs and pervy little fetlocks that looks as if it wouldn't support a plate of feathers, to a fat-armed geezer who'll upturn it and let his dog use it as a shit tray with scratching posts attached. Anything made with stripped pine she would piss on. Anything smooth she would like to gouge – the warm glassy patina of two hundred years of love in a safe, static environment, a table top that had cards played on it, hands held over it, contracts signed and books read on it – rake up its surface and rip out its history, which undoubtedly involved somebody's bondage. Sometimes, when she holds an old thing she gets a flash, a picture, like Beethoven, high on paregoric, riding his souped-up penny farthing into the local bathing pond.

Animals scuffle and squeal in the other room. Some of them have coloured marks on them to denote gender – it seems intrusive to keep picking them up to find out. Besides, it disturbs them. The dog experiment is not going well. It's not really happening. Of course, the research is all part of the act.

Someone is dumping more and more milk at her door. The last carton she threw dented the side of a van. Reg goes out to throw away another one and is hit in the face by a bunch of leeks.

"Fuck you!" she shouts.

The speeding minicab from which the missile was thrown screams to a halt and a familiar figure scrambles out, shouting, "Surprise!"

A headache is cresting in her but she takes Danny by the arm and drags him in. They nibble each others' hands before he slips into her from behind. She thinks of the ape and butterfly and tugs at his peach silk camiknickers, simultaneously cringing at them.

When he's gone, Reg's legs and arms ache as if boiling inside. She takes a tiny dab of the ointment and goes through the recordings of every session she's had with a client. The 20 hour tapes tend to get stuck. Touching them is like touching soap flakes, they seem to rub and dissolve in your hand. After using one, she holds her fingers against the rollers on an old tape player and hears a tiny chattering of sound, minute slices of time rolled together back on themselves like thin layers of ink. She rubs the tape all over her body and touches herself with vibrating electrodes. She plugs in eight speakers and strokes herself with the plastic receptor like an ultrasound probe. Waves of voices cascade round the flat. The sound fades easily, so she rubs and rubs until her skin is stained with sound, bathing in voices. Reg becomes comatose after a while, and wakes twitching with static, the voices used up. Her left hand shakes.

She sways around the lab, picks up a mother rat and suckles from her tiny nipples. She feeds her animals. *Love looks not with the eyes but with the mind.* She picks out a little white mouse who was born with no eyes and its brain exposed. It showed a strange reluctance to mate with the female Reg put in with it until it had got to know her. Then they built something together. Now they seem to be having a drink, or at least taking it in turns to suck from the tiny valved pipe, and then looking at each other.

But then there is a scream from the cage. The female mouse has drawn blood from the male's exposed brain and is consuming it while the male claws at her and screams, its tail stiffly curling, agonised. Reg takes a few polaroids before reaching for the chloroform but it's too late. The male lies twitching, dead. As Reg puts her hand in to take the body out the female, with dark pit eyes, runs up her hand and arm up to her ear where it tries to burrow its way in. She yanks it, tearing her own flesh in the process. She holds the mouse in her fist. It screams at her with a voice more human than a tiny rodent's. She forces it back into its cage.

There is a murmur in the corridor and a rustle of carrier bags. The neighbours are starting to complain about both the increasing numbers of hopeless women who queue to see Reg despite her increasing rudeness, and the random shrieks that torch the stairway's carpeted silence. It was raining the night before, so Reg has put down plastic for them to stand on. The old cow on the ground floor keeps getting woken out of her hangover sleep-offs.

The shuffling and chattering stops. Two sets of feet come up the stairs followed by a chorus of screaming and the sound of backs being flattened against the wall. There is a massive hammering on Reg's front door. Oh, go away.

Reg looks in the mirror, at her sweaty upper lip, and looks behind her at her screen. If she lets them all in at once she can get the treatment over quickly.

She peeks through the hole in the door. The crowd huddles in horror as Lucy and her mother come up the stairs. Reg opens the door to speak and hears Lucy say quietly from the top of the stairs, "Mummy, I forgot something." Lucy turns and the women, as one, charge down the stairs in a maddened shoal. The mother goes into her flat, comes out again, and leaves the building.

Lucy sits down on the stairs. She covers her face, as if hoping to hide herself from the air which sees everything, with its billions of tiny, free-flowing eyes. Seeing Lucy, Reg has a flashback to her own childhood of screams.

"Are you locked out?" says Reg.

"I'm not supposed talking to you."

"Why is that?" It's as if Lucy's mind has been crushed and crushed into an increasingly smaller space. It is giving off more and more energy, like a black hole. Lucy's button eyes are like black holes, too. She is smiling.

"What I is is me my pictures tell that my parents won't stop telling me to talk and now I don't know what to say 'cos when I open my mouth it's like wrong. Is it wrong to think?" Reg stands still on the landing. The little girl gets up and imitates her standing. She has become a petite mausoleum for a childhood that barely happened. It is so often this way with middle class children, tightly swaddled in the cotton wool of prevention, soft flesh rubbed raw when the effete cladding of their upbringing is slashed and burnt by real life. Reg knows what to say next.

84

"Do you like Fishyhugs?" Lucy's face lights up.

"I'm not allowed to eat them, but I had some at a friend's house once."

Back home, in fact, Lucy clamoured for them. She was met with a tirade about plebeian foods, shouted at, then slapped by her mother. In a final historic act, Lucy went out and spent her pocket money on some Fishyhugs of her own, which she skived off afternoon lessons at school to take home and cook. Unfortunately, she could not quite reach the old-fashioned grill-style unit, and had to throw the Fishyhugs up into it. One of them cleaved itself to the element and burnt with opal-hued incandescence before charring to a hard knot of processed matter that took Mr Towle an hour and a half's chipping to remove.

Lucy tells Reg how her mother was more angry about the presence of Fishyhugs in her home than Lucy missing lessons or the damaged grill. She alternately screamed at and hit Lucy until the walls rang and the china stoats on the mantelpiece shuddered.

Reg's laughter makes Lucy jump. Reg is doubled up over the bannister, hysterical.

"Come and see my flat, we can have all the Fishyhugs you like there." Lucy gets up with alacrity and follows Reg through the door. She walks round and round the huge rooms.

"It's so, it's so – fun!" shouts Lucy, rolling on the floor as Reg begins grilling. A massive organ blast strikes out from her main screen. Message overload. Reg feels menaced. She sits her small guest down and feeds her Fishyhugs, Spudniks and Blastic sauce, in massive amounts. Lucy eats like a little digger. She looks up and smiles.

"I like you." Lucy has already learned to twist her head down and to the side with her mouth staying locked open, lower jaw back, with that indirectness so many children take on when they learn that if they are direct they will be hit. Lucy appears to relax into a cushion, but her shoulders are still all upwards, as if relaxation was impossible. Reg leans forward, asking permission with a gesture, and undoes the top two buttons of Lucy's blouse. Lucy still instinctively moves only her eyes, as if greater movement would be punished. Reg feels kindness bloom out of herself. Pushing research to its limits, Reg asks Lucy to put a light on. Lucy approaches the switch like a nervous animal, grips it with delicate firmness and with infinitesimal slowness, and squeezes. It seems to take minutes to perform this simple action. Lucy notices Reg's incredulity.

"My mum screams at me if she hears me put the light on."

But Lucy will not stop smiling and her head is cocked in another way, as if she is concealing something. Her nervousness could almost be learned, not only from experiencing threats, but from learning to appear as if she were experiencing them.

Reg looks at the little girl. Could she impregnate her with a mouse's sperm? Or just combine the two on a slide? It would grow quickly enough in time for June 21st. She is horrified by her own thoughts.

Come and live here, be my familiar, Reg thinks. She takes a nice mouse from its cage and lets Lucy play with it.

"All my parents do is put things in boxes. Something is something, somebody is something, and then they've crossed them out. They never like people. What are you doing here with these animals?" Lucy asks.

"I'm working on a living exhibition that'll tell people what they really need to know about life. My genetic circus."

"What's that mean?" Lucy sits in front of her, her arms around her knees.

"Well, Lucy, you and me should really feel sorry for men. They've only got one X chromosome. We've got two."

"What's a chromosome? Is it like tits or something?"

"Well, kind of, but they're unimaginably tiny, and there's a whole set of them in every cell in your body, 46 in fact. So there's millions of them. Basically, they're like a living map of the human race. The sperm goes into the egg," Lucy *must* know about this, "and as soon as it does that, it starts something like a

– like when you programme a computer to make a picture, and then it draws it. And that drawing is a human being."

"But how does it know what to do?"

"Because we're alive. And if something's alive, it's got to be growing somewhere."

"But I thought we was all dying as soon as we're born. My parents keep on saying that to me. That's why I'm rubbish."

Reg twists her hair.

"You're not rubbish, Lucy. How can a ten year old girl be rubbish?"

"What's a sperm do then?"

Christ! She should have learned that at six.

"A sperm is your daddy's love letter to your mummy, and the egg is your mummy's mailbox where the letter goes, and then God comes to find it when they've gone out to work. And then he takes the letter and puts a baby in its place! A bit like the tooth fairy."

Why didn't Reg tell the truth?

"But I thought there was no God!"

"Lucy, for the purposes of this discussion let's take it as read. The history of philosophy is strewn with corpses where God's concerned. It's like a teleological roach motel."

Reg murmurs this last bit, and feels foolish.

"OK."

"The X chromosome is the strong one. It carries loads of information on it about what the person is going to be like, much more than the Y. Because the man has only one, anything he gets given must be passed on to him and the next generation. Genes carried on the X are called 'recessive' – are you following me?"

"No." Lucy bites into a Miniroll.

"Well, the point is that stuff on the X is often carried by women but affects far more men. Stuff like killer diseases, colour blindness and things." The feeble Y is no more than a castrated hieroglyphic of the X.

"There's this scientist, called Mary Lyon, who invented a theory about women's two Xs. If women had two, she thought, why didn't they get loads of the diseases themselves. She decided—"

Reg knows the woman would fume at her boiling down of her theory, but it's been bugging her for ages.

"She reckoned that in women, every pair of Xs has one switched off, she thinks at random, to achieve what's called 'dosage compensation', well anyway, to bring women down to men's level."

It is as if before every woman's eyes are two buttons, chunky, old-fashioned coloured light buttons from a fairground, one to press, one to leave alone. And the dwarf in the glass case above them spits out his response on a ticket that slipped down a tin chute and onto the ground. Yes or no, true or false, on or off, choice or no choice, love or hate, run or stay. A simple choice. The simplest binaries drive the impulse to life, and command the million armies inside every woman.

"Imagine if—"

"Can I have some more Fishyhugs?"

How to explain to Lucy that we are all suffering from classification. It started in the nineties. Journalism slowly began to disappear up its own arse in an orgy of self-referentialism. The first children of the mass-media age became old enough to write and broadcast about everything in their pasts until there was nothing more to repeat. Net freaks and mosaic thinkers began to philosophise so expansively that soon the most unattainably futuristic concepts, once the province of a few fiction writers, became commonplace and extremely boring, and were then used in advertising. Classification has destroyed dreams. Once you've imagined every organic molecule on the planet, that ever was and ever will be, able to commune in harmony, where else is there to go? Linnaeus wasn't to know that. Nor even Freud. But it won't really happen, not for a while anyway. God's made lots of firewalls. He's not stupid.

Spontaneously Lucy says, "I carved my mother in soap and squeezed her in the bath until she disappeared, *dead!"*

That was brilliant. Reg can use that in the show. She hands something to Lucy. Lucy waves the gun joyously.

Meanwhile, in a shopping centre somewhere just outside London, there is a scream. This shopping centre was the first in an outpost city made grand by industry and justified by a cathedral. It is a great, clean tank of soft sound next to the fumy winter air and coughing trees outside it. Families, some joyous, some bowed, filter up and down. Suddenly there is a crump, the sound of paper carrier bag on shiny ceramic. A female, 42, is rooted to the spot. A pair of children are ahead of her, running around and around a pillar. She cannot move past them. As she stands, people bump her like boats. The crowd soon begins to divide and flow around her, the bump rippling backwards to the doorway of the shop where people cannot tell what is happening.

"What's this dozy mare doing in everyone's way? It's the menopause! Oh no, she's too young for that."

Rigid she is, right next to a gift shop, surrounded by glass shelves and pastel neon framing atrocious pottery. The woman cannot move past these toy humans, these singing, sinning, dancing things, each small mouth a tiny crack of doom. And so she stays until Security moves her on.

She should never have gone to that bloody gypsy woman, letting her give her weird medicine. Better get a valium script from the GP.

"Sold out? How the hell can you be sold out?"

"Madam, all the tickets were sold out yesterday. It has become a popular destination just in the last few weeks. Odd really, it's still chilly at night, but then—"

"Oh for God's sake! I just want to get out of here. I'll stand."

The woman pushes her dark glasses up her face and starts to shake. She has left the school where she teaches without giving notice. Four other women see each other in the ticket hall and seem to know what unites them, except the one small detail which they will not want to reveal to a stranger just yet. The brackets that hold up the station ceiling are very thick.

"I can't go back there, I can't!" One of them is a WPC.

"Did you see what those little bastards did in Leyton Road? They crucified a lollipop lady right next to her crossing. Her eyes were all rolled up and funny and they cut off one of her hands! I mean why can't they just catch them and put them back in school? Kids in school are little angels!"

"I don't care about schools any more. Let's just storm the train!" The four of them pick up their Karrimors and bedrolls and run awkwardly to the train where they barge politely past the conductor and begin a sit-in in the dining car.

five

LUCY TAKES AIM AND FIRES. The screen blazes for a second and then flashes up a trophy. A voice says, "Congratulations! Stage One: 20 Avenge points! Already! But you've got a lot to get through, Lucy!"

There is a burst of bleeps and the screen darkens. *Blast The Past* reviews your childhood – decisions that were made, facts and fictions you were told – challenging you to relive incidents and remedy them with a special gun. It can be tailored to any number of variables and the outcome is always satisfying, with lots of bangs and electronic pleas for mercy.

Reg watches the child at the screen, observing the movements of the mouse-arrow flailing like a chain of cars on a rollercoaster. Lucy is learning fast, but then don't they all?

"What does it mean, Regina? Does that mean I'm brilliant?"

"Yes, of course it does!"

Lucy's parents keep telling her that her dyslexia is a sign of her innately useless brain and lesser talents. It's no good when a child starts thinking things are 'symbolic'. The ability to see things symbolically is an agony peculiar to the human race. While animals are capable of unhappiness, it is only humans who have the capacity to see beyond the immediate reason, which drains their energy and confuses them.

"Would you like to go shoplifting this afternoon?" asks Reg.

Reg feels this amateur act of gain is really far below her by now, but she feels she must initiate Lucy, as a father might take his beloved son to a prostitute.

The air is still cold. At first Lucy appears reticent, buoyed with moral water-wings. They sit on a bench along the road from the grocery, arguing.

"But it's wrong to take things that aren't yours."

"Who do you think that stuff belongs to?"

"The shop."

"No it doesn't. We all pay taxes. We owned all that stuff while it was still at the factory. And anyway, rules were made to be broken, Lucy. Rules are for scaredy cats."

"What if everybody broke them?"

"Most people don't, Lucy, because most people form the structure of society. Think of society as an enormous barbecue; most people are the dull grey bricks and charcoal. We need them to be there, because we're the flames. We burn, we transform things, we are the alchemical powers." Lucy pulls at her T-shirt with nerves.

Reg picks up a flyer from the ground. It has a big 'I' on one side. It is one of the special numbered ones given out by Pete Wolf, famous performance artist. 'I' is his favourite word. These flyers, if folded in a certain way, reveal a choice biographical detail about Pete, and guarantee you a front row seat at one of his shows.

Lucy sits, feet swinging just off the ground, in a posture of girly composure. Being brought up is like being drawn, over and over again. You are forced to copy what's around you until your arms, legs and mind fall into the same structure, and before you know it, you are imprisoned without the need of manacles. The uptight child is hated more by adults, far, far more than the child who is naughty, carefree and forgetful. And timidity is despised. The fearful animal who runs and hides under the sofa is soon ignored; the child who will not join in is soon kicked in the heart. The heart swells with pain and the child walks around for the rest of its life carrying this inflated organ, reacting to its every movement as a sign of grave illness. But perhaps Reg is not looking closely enough. There are splinters of tungsten in Lucy's eyes.

"I'm a horrible little girl. Everyone says so." Without a word, Reg marches her into the shop.

"Did you want any help?" asks the assistant, timeless in collared gingham pinafore. Well I did, thinks Reg, until a pasty-faced cow like you came along.

Until it is time to leave, Reg entertains herself and the assistant by guessing the woman's star sign. Lucy's got four tins of butter beans, a packet of J-cloths and some firelighters. They go back to Reg's for tea. Danny arrives, wearing a mob-cap and a dustbin liner. Lucy leaves.

On her way back into her parents home, Lucy trips on her skirt and her pocket falls open. Pills cascade around her. She is speedily furtive in picking them up. In her room, she draws them, hundreds and hundreds of them. It's the first time Lucy has used colour in a picture in her life.

"Lucywaddle, these are pretty," her father says about 20 minutes after he comes home from work. "What are they?"

"They're pills from that lady down the stairs."

"Pills? What did she say?"

"Nothing, she didn't give me anything."

"Yes, but what did she say to you? You mustn't associate with that sort of person. Wait till your mother gets home! We told you not to talk to vulgar people!"

"But the pills were pretty on the stairs—"

"I don't care about the pills! You mustn't talk to people like her. That's odd. The milk's off again." Lucy goes to see her pet mushrooms, the ones in the back corner of her wardrobe. She hears her mother arrive, a silence over the pill picture. Then she hears the deep thud of washing up.

"Lucy! Come down NOW!" Lucy goes down.

"We told you not to talk to her. Why did you do that?"

"But I—"

"Why did you do something we told you not to do?"

"I didn't."

"Don't answer back!"

Mrs Towle slaps Lucy around the face with a warm, wet washing up glove. The sting is like fire.

"Little cow! How did we end up with such a stupid, vulgar child? So naive as well. How could I have produced a child with so few street-smarts as this?"

Mrs Towle stands, theatrically, in the kitchen, hand on hip, looking down at Lucy who is trying not to clutch her face, knowing she will be hit again if she speaks, but suspecting she is just as likely to be hit again if she doesn't. The dog whines in the cupboard.

"I'm so bored of this child," says her mother, ripping up the pictures. "Why don't we change her?"

"I read somewhere that there's a special artificial adolescence injection they're trying to develop," says Mr Towle. "Perhaps we could give her that and get it over with as soon as poss!"

Mrs Towle shakes her head. Mr Towle farts and picks up a large book.

"I'm going off to the pot with some nudes," he giggles. "Oh, it's all right – it's art!"

Lucy smiles.

Later, at school, she receives her first ever compliment.

"Lucy Towle this is pretty! Lovely colours! Well done!"

The new teacher wants to think he has made a breakthrough with the little girl in the blouse who only makes white things, and has drawn only in white in the two weeks since he was drafted in to replace the previous teacher who has gone off on intemperate leave. These are pictures the little girl has done out of school, part of their 'home life' project. The project is destined to fail very soon, as the truth of what was going on in so many homes is really not suitable for general viewing.

The teacher is relieved at Lucy's quietness, although he has read somewhere that this type of 'goodness' is a sign of something more sinister. Since it is one less shining little demanding face bleating up at him, he is not going to waste time bringing her out. The other children keep their distance from her.

The new pictures are soft browns and reds, the browns ranging from hot ochre to chocolate black, smeared in fan shapes with curious pressure. They are also perfumed with something chemical. But then everything is chemical, even love; they taught the kids that ages ago. The little girl smiles up at him, "Pint of your best bitter my good man, and be quick about it!"

"Lucy! You've been reading! Good!" The teacher is getting used to spontaneity in children.

"Jesus wept, and the man was cured of his ankylosing spondylitis."

The little girl's eyes are shining, her voice soft enough not to be heard by anyone else, which should be a relief for the teacher, but terrifies him. Her face has an adult set.

"Put that down, you ugly little prick!" The teacher's smile wastes away.

Back in her room that night, Lucy tears down her photographs and sticks four blank sheets of paper on the walls in their place. Lucy stares into these rectangles and smiles. The door bursts open. Mrs Towle sashays in, her hand to her head, and sits heavily on Lucy's bed crushing two of Lucy's paintings.

"What am I supposed to do with a man like your father, a weak, silly man like that? Don't pick your nails, Lucy. You prefer me, don't you, Lucy, you're more like me, aren't you?" Lucy pinches the flesh on her wrist until it aches dully.

"Answer me, you prefer me, don't you?"

"I prefers me," Lucy recites, with banal intonation.

" 'Prefer', Lucy, not 'prefers'. Answer my question."

"I did."

"Don't answer back."

"I didn't." Lucy's hair splashes as her mother hits her. Mrs Towle stands up and screams for her husband. A long repetitive scream which should be thin with frustration but is suspiciously thick with healthy, muscular control. Lucy lets out a growl, a growl so deep it merely strums the airways. Mr Towle probably thinks it's her stomach.

Mr Towle trots up the stairs.

"Who gave her the bad genes?" *Who cut down the cherry tree?*

"It can't have been me, so who was it?"

"Well it wasn't me, dearie little bum." Lucy is sitting on the edge of the bed.

"Well it certainly wasn't me!" screams Mrs Towle. "I mean you do actually read the papers don't you. You do realise that soon they're going to be able to trace every single, bloody, fucking, shitting characteristic in every single human being. By God, you'll be up for the chop then, we'll all know the truth about you, my darling, your thin blood with iddly, tiddly little bits in it."

"Bitch."

"Did you hear that, Lucy! He called me a bitch! I don't believe it." Mrs Towle looks at Lucy as if she were a dying kitten.

"Where's your nice pictures, Lucy, your nice, little, square, funny ones?"

"I took them down."

"But why have you put blank pieces of paper up instead?"

"Because I wanted to."

"But why?"

"Because I did."

"Don't answer back." There is a sudden fart smell in Lucy's room, a lamb chop and greens fart which rises around them like fog. Mr and Mrs Towle leave the room and go down to watch television, during which Mr Towle puts his finger up Mrs Towle's behind and keeps it there for nearly an hour. He likes this form of union. It makes him feel secure.

Lucy walks round and round her room, back and forth through the fart's miasma as it faded, as if trying out a Bermuda Triangle that will not respond. She picks one of the mushrooms from the cupboard and draws on the window with it.

"Milk's off again!"

Lucy burns brightly in her room. She stays there, not eating, not drinking. The sun, warmer these days, dims to the sound of the news downstairs. She tries to listen for sounds coming from Regina's flat, but her hearing is only average, and anyway there are two storeys between them. Downstairs her parents shriek.

Lucy waits and waits for it to be dark. She wishes she had one of Reg's mice with her. She sits and sits, arms around knees. She puts the light out and the room flashes dark before slowly lightening again with the external glow. She does not cry.

Much later, early in the morning when the sun comes back, she walks with crusted eyes down to the sitting room. What a mess!

Lucy sets to work. Then she goes to the kitchen and waits for her parents to get up.

"Lucynob! Up early!"

"I cleaned up all the blood in the sitting room!" They look at her.

"Lucy. Are you mad?"

"There was bloodstains all over the place."

" 'Were', not 'was'."

"God I wish I had that funny new phobia everyone's talking about – we could put her in a care home!"

"There is no blood in this house."

"Reg. You've got mice, rats and a dog. Why don't you have a cat? You're a witch, aren't you?"

"Do you know the story about cats sitting on babies' faces, supposedly to keep warm, but actually they kill them?" asks Reg.

"Well, the modern version of that is that cats deliberately throw up on computer keyboards. There's been loads of stuff in the papers about it in the last few years. It's highly dangerous. You have to buy a new one if that happens. So no cats here Lucy, sorry."

"What about a monkey? Actually I'm glad you don't have one of them. They're too much like people. I think they should all be killed and fed to the Third World."

"You read my mind." Reg wishes Lucy would go and play, but she doesn't seem to know how.

"Tell you how you could help me, though."

Reg sends Lucy out on a mission. She wants to be alone. She is dreading the dinner tonight with Lou's friends, a womens' networking group. Argh. She never goes to dinners, but Lou begged her.

Since the car ban, central London has mellowed. Dispatch riders must alight and take their messages on foot. Businesses have made such a fuss about it that a half-hourly pigeon post is being considered. "Slow it all down!" is the motto and, secretly, everyone is pleased. Reg strolls through the little streets hardly noticing the brief drive of chilli-scented rain onto her.

Suddenly she is caught by a voice, sharp and sing-song above the feet and music of Soho.

"Regina!"

God, it's the Weasel Woman, an old colleague and part-time enemy, a soft voiced creature with a coil of dark brown hair. They have had many face-offs in their time, always understated, always balanced by the woman's acknowledgement of Reg's professional success, and Reg's of the woman's greater slyness. Reg has tried to get by on personality alone, yet she grudgingly admires this woman's control of things; the breathtakingly familiar remarks designed to unsettle; the sudden severe blanking of the face when an equally familiar question is asked in return, as if confidentiality were taken as read.

"So what did you get up to today, Niki?" It is hardly worth bothering to ask the question, since the response will be a pared down conflation of lie, exaggeration and assumed mystique.

"Oh, I did a few deals."

Sure, sure, you bought a pint of milk and ordered some newspapers, Reg nearly says. Reg always feels slightly generous in not dissecting Niki verbally. Where most of her money comes from is a mystery, but then that is the whole point. She likes to go and to have lapis beads plaited into her hair. Niki used to lead Reg on sexually. But of course, they never actually did anything. Thwarted by the state of being creative but without the talent to accompany it, Niki takes the weak and small and creates from them people in the image she requires for that day, week, year's satisfaction. She cannot get to Reg, and displays her dissatisfaction with the situation by coming out with sudden statements like, "Regina, you know, I know so much about love!"

Reg has looked up 'love' in the dictionary many times, but sees only lined, padded holes in flesh, flesh-ports for other flesh. People who discuss their loves too openly are suspect. Niki's protestations on love are mawkish and cloying, like fudge smears on a window. Niki's lovers are male, impressionable, runtish public schoolboys, desperate to experience the mythical side of life, seeing the ruby red walls of their mother's wombs in her velvet-draped love-box apartment. But Reg knows that behind the embroidery are patched, dampish walls with thin old emulsion on them. Perhaps, in the flat somewhere, stacked behind some distressed leather sculpture, is a cycle of paintings by a schizophrenic man in the last stages of illness, perhaps the woman's own brother. Reg always hopes that behind false people's façades lies something devastatingly real, but no-one has ever really proved it to her.

Regina's mother never painted or drew, at least not in Reg's lifetime. But she had once been an artist, until the day she thought she would become part of one of her own drawings.

She had said that if she made a line on the paper it would instantly connect with everything and that would be the surefire end of her.

Niki speaks, "Regina, I'm so happy. They came to the flat and bought everything I had! All that old Spanish stuff! So now I've gone all granite and blonde wood."

"Oooh, very nice," murmurs Reg, remembering her Spanish phase, with freezing, dusty wood floors and enormous, hideous dark wood sideboards. Just say the S-word and the chilly ugliness is miraculously transformed.

"Reg, you don't look very pleased for me!" Niki pouts at her for the last time, as it turns out. She vanishes, and all that remains of her is a weasel; whiskered, bright-eyed, narrow and suggestive in its movements. Reg strangles it and tosses it into a bin. That is Regina's third successful spell, although she does not realise it.

The bar is airy, with wood and metal fixtures, and low-key, although there is a lot of noise. Reg enters. Some people are arguing about the benefits of mixer taps. Reg moves up the stairs and knocks on a door to the private room. A small waiter in little round glasses peeps round the door and looks at her. He is fairly camp but has the grumpy demeanour of someone who cannot not quite bring himself to come out. Therefore, as a barman he is rude, and short changes people wherever he can.

Reg sits down next to a woman wearing wooden earrings and a navy blue fringed suede tabard. On the other side of her is a girl who rattles every time she moves. She is wearing a man's suit jacket; underneath it, a pink and black T-shirt bearing the legend "I Fuck A Lot" covers large breasts. She has huge calves from charity rock-climbing weekends, and a rigid coppery-red perm. She works as a marketing consultant for a counselling company.

"Hello. My name's Cathy. This is my first time! It's so nice to think there are people out there who're just a little bit wild like me. Are you famous?" Reg smiles. The woman babbles in a high, squeaky monotone.

"Ray, my boss, came past me yesterday and said 'Cathy, what's that clanking noise I hear whenever you walk around?' and I said 'Well, Ray, that's just my labial rings!' I think it's very important for women to express their individuality – all the magazines say so. And so does Johnny! Always time for a change, eh! What was your name again?"

"Regina."

The static ripples of her hair are like gigantic grooves in a record.

"It's unbelievable," says Wooden Earrings, "you can't open a cereal packet these days without finding a pair of handcuffs or a miniature gag. I blame the media! I mean, people are making passes at cats, dogs and even children!"

"Obviously, I like to go with a woman now and again," I Fuck A Lot goes on, "because that's really cool, and womens' sexuality is very different from mens'."

She pauses to re-draw a dark mahogany line around her lips.

"You know," she exclaims suddenly, "I've been to every single EU country apart from Denmark, Portugal, Spain, Luxembourg and Germany!"

"That's like saying, if it wasn't for your arms and legs, you'd have no limbs," says Reg.

"Ooooh ha ha! That's quite good! And it's true as well!" She giggles. "Wow! Women are just so cool about their sexuality! You know, my boss asked me the other day, 'Cathy, guess how much I weigh?' and I said, 'You'd know if the dial on my forehead didn't always get so steamed up!'"

More women arrive, taking the number to 12. A famous psychoanalyst and media personality arrives. She has the movements of an ex-dancer and is wearing a long, trailing chiffon scarf. Someone pours Regina some wine. She already has two glasses within her sight that no-one has claimed. The famous psychoanalyst nods graciously at her with a look of the one in charge.

"You're Regina, I understand."

"Yes."

"Lou tells me you're a – therapist, of sorts."

"Of sorts, yes."

"I must say I'm not aware of you. You're quite an outsider."

"Yes, I am." Reg smiles. The famous psychoanalyst turns to the man next to her without another word.

Isadora Duncan's wheel, where are you now when I need you? thinks Reg. There is a knock at the door. The table falls silent, as if the people there are taking a few moments to compose themselves. Knives are laid carefully to rest while mouths are wiped and available hair fluffed around the edges of faces. As the visitor is let in they begin eating again so as to be able to look up in pleasant surprise at their new companion. It is Lou. Reg's eyes open wide. She cannot help it.

She is wearing strange, enormous sunglasses. Reg notices that magazines and any other conduits of visual art are covered or hidden. Lou gestures to Reg with watery enthusiasm and takes her coat off in front of them, revealing a black suit.

"So, no-one else has succumbed yet!" There is a round of mental self-crossing, heads raised from mousse in pretend enquiry, as if to encourage her to drop the subject.

"It's all become too much, everyone. I've chanted and chanted, but it was when I went to a friend's house and someone brought their children with her. I was just chatting, having a lovely time talking about growth, when one of the little monsters appeared in the doorway asking for a refill of apple juice. I slammed myself against the wall, screaming. It was all so embarrassing. I just can't look at them. I just can't!"

Wooden Earrings interrupts her.

"A friend of mine was feeling a bit insecure a few weeks ago and went to see some woman in a flat somewhere, who sold her some funny ointment, or something, that made her feel, well, a little bit *high*," she giggles. "Ever since then she's been ranting about children and how much she detests them. I mean, sorry Lou, I know *you'd* only go to Johnny if you had a problem, but it does seem a bit strange. A bit of a coincidence."

"I know someone who did that too!" says I Fuck A Lot. "I found her crouched down in a bus shelter! I said to her, 'If you're looking for a shag, you won't find one here!' and she told me all about this weird medicine woman."

Reg looks down. The door opens and the meal begins.

Deep bowls piled high with mussels in juice are brought by a sullen beanpole wearing black. She is probably a resting actress, perhaps unaware, in the arid fug of her mind, that if she cannot even act the part of a waitress, let alone play out the tremendous emotional gamut of being respectful to the punters, she will never get a place at drama school. She pushes stray elbows and cigarette packets out of the way as she thumps the bowls on the table.

"Mools!" squeals I Fuck A Lot. They begin to eat. But what should be firm, succulent ochre mouthfuls, peeping coyly from glossy, bearded shells, are soft, crumbly yet strangely greasy primrose-coloured things, like the tongues of diseased dwarves, a handful of which could probably light a childrens' bedroom for several hours. Still, this is England, so people eat up, saying repeatedly to each other, "You did well there!"

The starter, which everyone manages to get some way through, is taken away and replaced with some dainty slabs of chicken breast, in a lemony creamy sauce, with a lump of spinach. The chicken is so undercooked that each rasp of the knife squeezes forth a wash of rosy fluid, thickened by a suspension of antibiotics and scarlet threadlets of tissue.

Then they move on to coffee, via some very dry gateau with greasy caramel icing that sticks to the roof of their mouths. There is another coded knock at the door. The table goes quiet again. Lou looks irritated. Her hosts' friends are evidently dropping like flies and she will soon lose her cachet.

The new arrival is let in. This time it is a man, dressed in normal clothing and carrying a densely packed sports bag. A tiny, ecstatic thrill passes round the table and people begin discreetly fumbling for their wallets. He empties the bag on the table.

"These are some of the last remaining antiques in free circulation! Soon there will be none left, gone with everything that made England great, like the smell of uncleaned wet wool coats, or horse manure lining the streets. Our noble heritage will be reduced to historical fantasy and sold to fucking foreigners."

On the table are: egg-cups; enamelled boxes; reassemblable étagères; pinchbeck étuis; fairings; fob-chains; owl jugs; crab-shaped jelly-moulds; lace-maker's globes; pap boats; a life-size pewter weasel with electro-gilded gorse bush; a miniature enamel of a capercaillie; assorted treen (pill-silverers in particular); decoy ducks and trivets.

Reg feels sick. Everyone round the table seems to be feeling sick. It is said that to be ill is a safe way of expressing anger. So, when you are poisoned by bad food in a restaurant, your consequent vomiting is a safe way of expressing your desire to maim or kill the proprietor and chefs. You get a cold, you're mildly irritated about something; you get shingles, you're pretty fucked off; you get cancer, and your family'd better start packing, because you're really mad. Lou starts sneezing. She leans forward with her head against the table. Then she raises it again and her forehead is emblazoned with a stigmatic red strip.

"I can't believe it! I'm going to throw up!" I Fuck A Lot retches suddenly. Everyone is asking each other if they are all right. Reg leaves soon after.

When she gets back, Lucy has left a note.

rejina
I did wot U said and walked a bout in front of sum wimin. Some ov them screamed a bit and sum ran awa. i wos a bit skard but it did not botha me much at all rely. Ar they ill or somfin? Dont forget wot U sed abut more FishyHugs. I wod rely like a cat but me mum might kil it but she keep tellin me thats wot i'd do.

from me (lucy upstez)

Regina twists in her bed, her sheet wound around her so tightly that she feels like a pillar. In the dream, she is kneeling by a pool in the desert, drinking from it and, too late, sees the creatures below the surface. With devilish speed they begin to leap into her mouth. She throws her head back, but they only arc higher. They merge with her insides, harden and fuse her to the ground. She suddenly finds herself standing upright, her mouth frozen open. She stands in the sun. Some people come. From her mouth flows a stream of blood, the sound thick as the liquid drives into the pool. There are other, deeper splashes as the foetuses that burst from her fall into the water. The people do not seem to mind, and drink from her.

She wakes up in slippery darkness softened by tiny sunbursts as her eyes fight sleep. The dream has left her feeling suspiciously positive considering that its central image was a stream of bloody, half-formed babies pouring out of her mouth. She wishes for a consumer helpline. She imagines calling the Samaritans and getting a hapless student counsellor on his monthly shift. "I tried to bind metal with flesh! I tried to make it fly!"

A bell rings heavily in the street. The Krishnas sing with certainty, their voices jumping a little as they step over rubbish bags. Reg shivers.

Her sheets bind her feet.

At school the next day, Lucy proudly shows her paintings. Her teachers look at each other, frowning. One of them lifts the rippled paper to her nose and inhales. Intoxicated with suspicion, he holds the paper up to the light then offers it to the other teacher for analysis. Neither are in the mood for discussion; the other children are fighting, ganging up, fiercely proclaiming sexualities that change as fast as their allegiances. Francestina Skaggs has taken to wearing hats and a lot of make-up. Her friends crowd and murmur around her.

"Why so much red, Lucy dear? And so much brown? Put in some nice blues and pinks, and green grass." Half the children draw straggly hanging baskets when asked to represent the countryside, the others dog turds and litter or psychotic farmers killing small animals. Lucy just carries on the same.

"How clever though, you've made a quill pen and drawn pretty patterns with it."

There is a heavy silence.

"Lucy dear, come here." Suddenly Mr and Mrs Towle are there in the corridor, looking at her.

"How could you? What's wrong with you."

"Nuffin."

"THE WORD IS 'NOTHING'!" the Towles roar in unison.

Lucy's paintings are executed entirely in shit and blood; her mother's menses, extracted from forgotten tampons, and her own blood from razor blade cuts. In the past, Lucy never realised it would be cool and wild to show her cuts to the other children to get their respect. She might have expected a beating there and then, under the pitying eye of the highly embarrassed teacher who had first spotted the change in the lingering perfume of Lucy's works.

"We have to be understanding. Our child is ill," says Mrs Towle. She waits until they are in the car to hand out the appropriate punishment.

"What do you think you have made us look like in front of all those other people! Think what the other children will tell their parents! That we have a nasty, dirty little girl for a daughter; a mad, bad, sad little person who's never going to grow up, who is weak, and, as far as I can see, is actually very boring by the standards of children today. This little girl can't even rebel properly. She gets ill every time there's a sex education class at school. She doesn't even try drugs. What have we spawned here? I don't particularly want it!"

On the way up the stairs, Lucy breaks away from her parents, tears up to Reg's door and hammers on it.

"Help, help! Regina!" Reg appears in the doorway.

"Ah! Just the person we need to talk to!" calls Mrs Towle. She marches up to Regina, who shuts her door behind her and stands in the corridor, arms folded.

"You've been influencing our child, haven't you? You've been turning her brain! Answer me!" Mrs Towle insists they all go upstairs for a coffee.

When they get there, Mr Towle instantly retires to his study. Mrs Towle turns on Radio 4 very loudly.

...you have ten seconds left on 'grammar', starting NOW.

My grammar is a charming old woman, who used to take us to the lovely Peachey Smith's Museum of Beauticians' Errors...

Mrs Towle clashes the cups together as she dumps them on the table. A tiny chip flies up and hit Reg's cheek. There is a loud bang and Reg is surprised to see a large sheepdog skittering uncertainly on the parquet vinyl. It seems to be running on the spot, waste movements jerking it in all directions, head busking in crazed semaphore as it lurches towards Regina.

...the apple is a jolly sort of fruit and very versatile; you can bake it, roast it, fry it, boil it, rape it.

Interruption! You can't wrap an apple! Well, wrap it in what, may I ask, unless you mean of course encase it in millefeuilles?...

"What an interesting sweater, Regina. But then, with your dark colouring you can get away with it! I always say to my little girl, girls like her shouldn't wear black, it doesn't match her skin tone. I knew black doesn't go with my complexion so I went straight for navy blue and pink and I looked warm and beautiful and got married immediately.

"Now look. We know you've been talking to our daughter, but we must tell you that she isn't well. In fact she never really was. And I don't think you should be making it worse by influencing her. She doesn't know how to think for herself, you see."

Mrs Towle pushes the dog with her foot. It looks beatifically at her.

…must make you aware of the French verb raper, to grate…

Mrs Towle turns it up further.

…are you sure you didn't mean 'to rape' in a French accent?

'No no, that would be 'violer'…

The faceless paintings hang at the corner of the stairs, in bathrooms, and in the kitchen. Reg sits in silence, the light from the broad windows studio-like in its brilliance. She gets up and leaves. Lucy runs after her, begging Reg not to leave her. Reg takes Lucy by the hand and leads her down to her flat. There is the sound of a door banging as Mrs Towle follows them down the stairs. The radio blares and hisses with the twisting aerial as it xylophones against the bannisters. Mrs Towle storms into Reg's flat.

"You are influencing my child! What are you, some kind of witch?"

The radio shouts.

"Lucy, get back home. I'll deal with you later."

Mrs Towle squares up to Reg. Lucy shrinks behind her.

"She's nice to me! Not like you!" Lucy shouts. She darts out, picks up the radio and rams it at her mother's knee. Her mother falls to the ground. Regina holds Mrs Towle's arms behind her back.

"Now, what would you like me to do with her?" she asks Lucy.

"Kill her!" Lucy shrieks. Reg thinks very fast, then shouts at Lucy to go into the lab and get the white mouse with the red cross on it, but to put a glove on first. Lucy moves faster than she ever thought she could.

"Hold it tight!" shouts Reg, holding down Mrs T with all her weight. "Now take the mouse and hold it by her ear, right up close." Lucy does so. As soon as she loosens her hold on the mouse, it slips out with the speed of a snake and burrows into Mrs Towle's head. Mrs Towle gives a terrible long drawn-out screech as the mouse consumes her brain. One of her eyes bulges as the creature works its way towards the light.

"Is it a boy or a girl mouse?" asks Lucy.

"It's a girl," says Reg. "Don't let it get away. It's the only one I've got that'll do this. It's third generation, my first real success."

Bloody matter runs from Lucy's mother's other ear. Reg hopes it will not stain the floor.

"Serves you right!" shouts Lucy, who has tucked her legs up on her chair, but seems only to be going through the motions of being frightened at the execution. Reg, overcome with a fastidious disgust that surprises her, realises that she's been here before; except, the first time the creature eating her own mother's brain was imaginary, and the screams did not stop.

They pick up Mrs Towle before rigor mortis sets in and put her in the freezer, or The Ark as Reg calls it. This is better than anything she could have imagined.

The sun blasts into the speeding box that is taking Lucy and her father away from London and up the country, northwards, to a special school in Northumbria. Lucy does not know, but the Towles took out Difficult Child Insurance a long time ago. Lucy sits in the back, the smell of the interior sickening. There is no comfort against the sticky seats as the scent of old stains rises up. The Towles' car is filthy. There is a bloom of old animal hairs on the seats; tacky licks of orange juice have marbled the dashboard. They've been wiped away many times, but the residue remains. Occasionally Mr Towle tells Lucy to get her feet off the seats, as if he is about to collect a ticket from her. He does not seem to care where his wife has got to. He seems to think she has gone on one of her sudden 'therapy weekends'.

He doesn't really want to drive all this way, what with his shingles. His daughter has been painting pictures with his wife's menstrual blood and shit. Probably some tribe does it somewhere, he doesn't know. But really it's time to get rid of her.

Lucy needs to go to the toilet, and yet cannot face the agony of the search for a service station, achieving the slip road, parking, locking, mumbling about who has or has not wound up the window the half inch or so from the top, and whether first to have a clear-out of the cartons, wipes and softened newspapers from the back. Then, finding the toilet, Lucy is a bit nervous about the big groups of foreign schoolchildren with their caramel skins, largeness, good quality thick cotton clothing, expensive sunglasses, and voices with such a very different timbre to her own. They constantly commit terrible violence for an instant before moving on, laughing. It is what they will oblige her to do to them which irritates her.

But they do stop. Lucy goes to the toilet. She nearly makes it, but as she returns a huge French boy clips her while his smaller companion is trying to break one of his legs. Lucy falls against a small bushy sapling, raking up the top layers of skin on her arm and tearing her T-shirt. She hangs for a second, her arm stuck in the tough lower branches while the rest of her dangles, her hair stringing over her face.

There are loud foghorn giggles from the French children. They crowd around, blocking out the sun so it is almost cold, talking very fast and laughing like machine guns. They are at the age where there is a vast difference in size between children, huge deep voiced thugs with tiny squeaking minstrels bouncing around them. Incandescent flashes of sunlight between their shoulders catch Lucy's goose-pimples. One of the larger, older boys begins to rub his crotch frenziedly and there is another tide of giggles as Lucy tries to separate her hair from the branches of the thin tree. She doesn't want to look at their broad faces, alive with a purposeless, animal force that is capable of wrecking anything with one thoughtless jostle. As the little crowd becomes denser, they begin pushing. There are tiny silences as some of the boys begin to get bored. There is an adult murmur. Their two teachers are chatting and comparing nail varnish. Lucy gets up slowly from the tree.

A group of girls from the same party cackle nearby. The largest one is offering to be chased by two older boys who stand by, uninterested. She honks and squeals until the boys, barely looking at her, push her to the ground. Her skirt flaps up over her hips, revealing knickers whose bright purple flower pattern is stretched into mauve ovals. The distraction gives Lucy the chance to escape.

Mr Towle has parked in the far corner of the car park and is eating a scotch egg with designer mustard. A friendly family from Lancashire share their water and offer Mr Towle a beer. Mr Towle declines with a small-mouthed smile Lucy sees only rarely, when he is getting rid of someone from Save The Children. He turns to Lucy as if she were an adult.

"Nice day today, isn't it?"

Lucy says nothing.

"Lucy, you're a very rude little girl. I don't know what we did to deserve this sort of child. In fact—"

"Yes, it is a nice day today, isn't it."

"Lucy! How many times have we told you not to interrupt. That's what arrogant, bossy little girls do, and your personality isn't strong enough to be like that."

He gets into the car and shuts the door. The kids in the next car play and fight, circling in the dust and shouting. Mr Towle sniffs his fingers with a delicacy, an understated grace. The sun slips in and out of the clouds. Lucy slides through the gap in the seats like a snake, leaving one leg in the back so that her legs are spread. The velour is itchy under her.

"Daddy, why don't you get your cock out and I'll suck it for you!" Mr Towle looks at her in amazement tinged with possibility, and makes a sudden movement. Lucy has already spotted the fruit knife, sitting by the gearstick. In the same second, she grabs the knife and plunges it into her father's upper leg, straight into the femoral artery. Those old anatomy books they kept in the toilet, although she could barely read the simplest words, spoke to Lucy clearly through images and arrows.

Lucy gets out of the car and shuts the doors. The family leaves. She takes whatever money she can find on her father's body and walks back towards the service station. There is a honk from the French bus. The children begin to move, their energy temporarily sapped. Lucy sees the luggage compartment open and slips in, leaving her father's jacket caught in the door. How hard can it be to survive 50 miles in there after what she has done?

The coach stops in Edgware. Lucy crawls to the back, takes a lighter and holds it over a group of carefully stored carrier bags. There is some duty-free rum, wrapped up, which she opens, drinks, spits out and then pours around. The luggage door is flapped up and one of the teachers pulls away the jacket.

"Help, help!" murmurs Lucy.

The teacher swears and beckons her. Lucy feigns terror and keeps pointing to something even further back inside. The teacher crawls in, whereupon Lucy lights the bags, scrambles past the teacher and out into the blinding air. She shuts the door quietly. As she is about to run she sees that the key to the luggage compartment is in the lock. She turns it, takes it and walks away, slipping unnoticed along the side of the coach. She goes to find the Tube.

six

Reg is excited at having Mrs Towle motionless in her freezer. Even sedated, her own mother fought an invisible enemy.

Reg takes a call from a woman at Waterloo Station who is leaving her family and is demanding to know what the drug was Reg gave her. Reg flannels. The doorbell rings. She only answers it because the ring is coded.

"Pisces – I can smell it! With Virgo rising!" says Reg sardonically to herself. Reg looks down at Lucy, her lips in a half snarl.

"Why aren't you in Northumberland?"

"Oh, Dad decided not to do it in the end, so I've come back." Reg is suspicious.

Lucy eats waffle nuggets and black pudding, plays several rounds of KYP and smokes half a cigarette.

"How did the egg get its shell? How is the sky blue? How did the apple stay alive?" asks Lucy, gripping her knees. For God's sake ask about sex, thinks Reg.

"Well, one day the Jones family threw a French Golden Delicious out into their garden, where it lay under their own apple trees for weeks and weeks. Autumn turned into winter, and still it lay, never changing, while the Jones's apples fell, were holed by wasps and birds, and rotted. One of the children swore he'd seen it glowing in the dark. When, one windy evening, they went to look at the apple, neither insect nor bird had touched it..."

Lou phones.

"Reggie you were so naughty to leave early the other night. You were supposed to be networking! I couldn't believe it. It was pure denial."

"So, aren't you angry with me?"

"Of course not. It was all about you. It wasn't my responsibility. Anyway, I'm just calling to tell you that I can't take any more of my illness. I'm leaving town. There's a lovely place called Silver Camp where I'm going. Johnny's been really understanding about the kind of person I am and says he just knows I'll be fine for money while I'm there."

Lou sounds in pain. Her voice is strained and high as if all the red meat has been pulled from her throat and substituted with old, strandy veal.

Lucy is roaring around the sofa. She points at Reg and suggests, in a measured voice, "You're being punished for being weird and having men and women in your bed!"

Reg shakes her head. She can't handle Lucy around the house now. She wants to work. Lucy will have to go on another errand. Reg sends Lucy out to the Market to find some IVF micro-needles. They'll sell them to a child up there, no worries. Lucy sets off without a murmur, minipack on her back like Pigling Bland going off over the hills and far away.

Reg watches her go down the street. There is a nervy element to the heritage displays this morning. Lucy has to wait while a petulant Henry VIII clashes churchwardens with a fellow statesman while posing for a photo. As their voices become more belligerent and the pipes clash, Lucy barges through the little group, her pack bouncing on her back. She nudges spitefully at the King's stomach. He prods her in the back. Reg hears his curse from three floors up.

Ten minutes later the phone rings again.

"Just making sure you were in," someone says. God, Danny again. But it is not Danny. It is Phil, Jamie and two large geezers.

"We hear you've been having problems, Regina."

One geezer goes into the lab.

"Excuse me, but where do you think you're going?" Reg walks towards him. And then realisation hits her.

"Ohhhh, wait a minute. I get you, I get you!" She flops down in a chair and swigs from her mug of tea.

"Fuck's sake, we're all at it, aren't we? Brilliant!"

They look at her blankly.

"All right, all right, it's a fair cop, guv. Us artists, we're all in it together, aren't we. Christ!" They do not respond. The geezer comes back.

"Fuckin' 'ell. Look at that! She's got animals in cages 'ere, and a dog with something stuck on its back!" His voice is bass and rumbling.

"Cruelty to animals, Reg, that's not going to look very good, is it?"

"Yeah, yeah," says Reg, "sit down then. Have a drink."

"Oooh no, you're in it far too deep now. It's going to take a lot more than that to shut us up," says Jamie.

"Loony cow, probably got a body in the freezer an' all!" says the geezer.

"Oooh! Very good accent that, straight out of central casting!" she giggles.

"And where have you sent that little girl, that poor little girl, then?"

"What little girl?" To be honest, this is starting to sound dodgy.

"You've just sent her somewhere, haven't you?"

"What?"

"You heard us Reg. Old Harry VIII down there stuck a transmitter on 'er back so we'll know exactly where she is."

Reg is still giggling.

"Are you filming this?"

Jamie sighs theatrically, casts his eyes to heaven and pulls out a small handset.

"Wow! You've had some lottery money! OK OK, yes you can work with me on my next project!" sighs Reg, with a superior smile.

"You're very young to be walking about down here, little lady. What's your name?"

"That's none of your business!" Lucy's voice comes out of the gadget.

Reg wonders at the funding behind this particular stunt.

"Call yourself a human being, Reg, sending a fucking ten year old down the Market. A quick call to Mairead at Social Services should sort you out."

"Nah, Benjy'd be better. He's a real stickler for kids' rights."

Phil folds his arms.

"We're off now. If you don't keep your gob shut, you'll never see her again."

They leave, loudly.

"Harty, you were saying—"

"Yeah, Phil, you see, the thing is, as I see it, if it wasn't for the Nazi holocaust, communism would still have as bad a name as fascism. Fascism's been demonised well out of proportion. Remember the gulags, Stalin's purges—"

"Yeah, but—"

Reg sits, wondering. Maybe they're Situationists. Maybe they're not.

A bus ride gets Lucy to the gates of the Market. As a shopping centre, it was once a thriving focus for the local community but, as other rival malls became more prominent, someone decided it should become a national monument. During the brief, legally fallow period between its redundancy and projected redevelopment into a railway terminal, an army of homeless people rose as one and, carefully led by a group of less materially insecure people with mobile phones, moved into it.

It was not long before natural selection separated the truly subjected from the real operators, but somehow the two managed to achieve symbiosis. Those who wish merely to exist and form a nominally political community under one roof are free to do so. They make good use of the kitchens and keep the place clean. Those who wished to trade, legally or not, are equally free.

The local council has tried to evict the inhabitants. But it is hard to get rid of five hundred people plus visitors without the use of explosives or gas. When council spies reported back that there was a thriving cultural ecosystem that had started to get mentioned in the more 'out there' travel guides, the bureaucrats backed off, only occasionally organising some harassment.

No benefits are given to anyone who lives there, the council's side of the deal for letting them stay. Doll's legs, cracked television tubes and splitting broom handles have not been sold on such a large scale since the Russians fled into Europe. Software too, the new lines that never quite achieved mass acceptance, like *Learn to Drive on CD-Rom* and *Design Your Own Proverb!* It is also becoming a ghetto for performance artists too afraid to work elsewhere.

Despite the window boxes, crafts and philosophy, it is still a dangerous place. It has its own PR, with stories of hideous attacks in the vicinity. Its relative isolation means that a lone visitor is liable to be staked out for later consumption. So, the place remains credible, fashionable even, while inaccessible to the timid.

Lucy looks over the stalls. The medical suppliers are popular. Doctors with a conscience offer their services in the cubicles behind them. Lucy does Reg's shopping without a hitch, drawing attention to herself only by her politeness to the slightly hassled young doctor who kicks the needles to her under his table. Usually kids just snatch and run.

117

As she is walking away someone comes up behind her.

"Christ, I didn't even know they still used these. Kim, come and have a look. Sweetie did you know you had a bugging device attached to your bag! Where on earth did you get that from?" The woman's face is nice. She pulls the tiny object off Lucy's bag and holds it out.

"The things kids think are fashionable these days!"

"You can have it for a score," says Lucy, formally.

"Oooh! Fifteen, you little hustler!"

"OK then." The woman gets out some coins, a strange expression on her face. Lucy shrugs as she disappears.

The body piercers-in-training provide entertainment of a sort. Once piercing emerged from its exclusive barracks, it fast became the province of sales reps and trainee journalists. After the first Sunday supplement frisson, anyone could, and did, get a discreet gold or silver ring in their navel or nipple. First brewers, then car makers used this motif to advertise themselves. It was not long before manufacturers jumped on the bandwagon:

(All coyly naughty.)
Woman in office: *"I've got one."*
Man in city suit in street: *"I've got one too!"*
Teenager queuing at cashpoint: *"So have I!"*
Old lady in sitting room: *"And so have I!"*
Male Voiceover: *"Is it this?"*
(They all flip through cheque books.)
Male Voiceover: *"Is it this?"*
(They all lift their tops to reveal pierced belly button, penis, nipple or labia.)
Male Voiceover: *"No! They've all got a Nutley's carpet in their homes!"*

It was the final straw for piercing's cult status. But still, it's fun to watch them and their still defiant community of followers, just like the few punks who stuck around long into the eighties as earnest postcard fodder.

Animals cry out. Lucy opens a door and looks behind it into a small hall. There are cages but this is not a zoo. Stray dogs and cats are taken in here and redistributed among the loving. But many of them are still unwanted. They bear the hallmarks of breed-overload. There are hairless dogs, cats with legs so short their bellies are calloused, dish-faced Pekes, the lower half raw from the constant wash of mucus from the two buried nostrils, and rabbits whose ears are twice the length of their bodies. These animals have never been loved by anyone. They are the product of theory, and their own parents were too disgusted even to eat them. Lucy thinks of some of the things Reg has done in her lab. For ages Reg had been trying to mate blind mice to see if love really looks with the mind. They did breed so she began mixing them with sighted mice.

"The apocalypse trembles in its cage when the river of life is poisoned by hobbyists," Reg always says, sagely, before putting them to sleep.

A watchful man is steaming bowler hats in an alcove. From a distance the scene seems quaint, but there is something odd about it. She walks towards him. There is a bowl of very cute kittens beside him on the ground. It feels strange to see a normal animal. All Lucy has seen recently are twisted things. These kittens seem airbrushed, designed, unreal.

" 'Ello darlin', d'yer like my 'ats?" his voice falls to a whisper. "They're coming out in the summer, just before the school 'olidays." He smells of cigarettes.

Lucy realises the hats are two-thirds adult size or smaller. She thinks of the Steals, and what they will be wearing soon.

"Don't tell anyone, will yer."

There are cafés everywhere in what were once shops, sweetly old-fashioned, full of books, inviting intellectual discussion with a stranger in a non-judgemental environment. Lucy has seen a few books. Of course, schools still use them as teaching aids, but they have an audacious, wasteful structure, all that information gathered so clumsily. They are no more than souvenirs of civilisation; a man might beat someone to death and still have one in his pocket.

Lucy sits down and is instantly joined by two shaven-headed, middle-aged men in grey shirts. They look at her hard, and exchange glances. Someone puts on some music, sharp and bangy.

"Get a load of Dave's oldies—"

"That one's been out a week at least."

"You here on business, then?" one of them asks Lucy.

"No," says Lucy.

"Cute little kitties over there. Does your aunty, you know, have any pets?"

"I don't have an aunty."

"Maybe she's not your aunty then, that lady next door?"

"What lady next door?"

The man looks impatient.

"You do have a lady next door who's got dogs 'n' stuff. I bet you do?"

The look on his face tells Lucy to get away. She gets up and disappears into the crowd. There is a scrape of chairs as the men get up, too. As Lucy starts to run, a boy, no more than nine, taps her on the shoulder and rasps, "Real Es, like the old days!" He takes two pills and rams them down her throat with his salty fingers. Lucy gags heavily and regurgitates the tabs, her coughs high and squeaky. The boy grabs them off the floor and runs away.

Lucy pushes through the people and hides in the crowd. An ex-government ice-cream trolley passes her. There is no disguising such a familiar icon. People nearby wince in disgust. A tired-looking girl in a baggy brown sweatshirt halts drearily in front of her and starts handing out leaflets. There are protests somewhere as Lucy's pursuers shove people aside. A small crowd has gathered. A man appears above their heads and begins to speak, in a querulous, hectoring tone.

"I bought a pack of 12 batteries for the price of ten. I got them home and put two of them in my radio and they lasted less than a third of what they usually do!"

"That's outrageous!"

"Off yer chest!" an overcoated barker shouts. Lucy looks at the woman next to her. She is gaunt, her hair sitting in a flat black helmet. Her forehead is sheened, her nose dotted with tiny droplets of sweat, magnifying each blackhead. It is a cold day for April. Lucy looks at this woman and thinks that maybe she is a witch too, like Regina. Maybe she knows how to heal the sad, screaming women Reg is so worried about.

The woman has not noticed Lucy; her eyes are fixed on something at 2 o'clock from her, ten feet away and gaining. A small child, looking for its mother. It has a resigned look on its face, as if doing the same thing it had done a thousand times, like tirelessly mouthing a nursery rhyme. *Mummy where are you, mummy where are you.* The woman's eyes begin rolling, like those of a dying horse in a painting. The child locks onto her.

"Mummy!" it shrieks, interrupting a speech about a faulty suitcase padlock. She turns and runs. Lucy follows. The woman is fast. She darts up some stairs and onto the upper concourse, where the fortune tellers work, plying their trade at a trestle table or, if lucky, in a cubicle. Tossing down a few cards, pressing a few buttons on a rudimentary computer, probably adapted from one of those old 'How big is your sex drive' machines where you put your hand on a plastic pad, put in 20p and a pointer waved up and down and said whether you were Too Hot To Handle or just a Cold Fish. Or maybe gutting pigeons in front of a client and tossing their coiled entrails around. These sad luck traders were Reg's fleas. That's what she had said to Lucy.

Lucy catches the woman rushing through a doorway. On a large placard are the words: "Child-free zone. Please respect our rights."

The women here are cold and poor, mostly homeless until they called this home. Lucy peers into the room. A woman sits on a stool across the room from the bed. Lucy sees the glint of small bottles in a row beneath it.

"Fuck," says the woman, throwing herself down on the bed, which is so soft it folds into a V shape, the blankets swarming around her waist. The woman, shaking, shiny like a roast, rolls up her sleeve and reaches over to a box with a cloth over it. Her arm is rutted with bruises and scars.

She pulls off the cloth to reveal a cage. When the dog inside sees her it leaps up and begins wagging its tail sweetly, its ragged face smiling upwards. But as soon as she opens the cage door, it springs forward and takes her arm in its teeth with a vicious grip. The woman trembles and raises her head. Beatification flowers in her face as the animal gouges her flesh. The woman sobs with relief as the blood weeps through her punctured skin.

"I hate children! I hate them so much! Why are there so many of them?"

She looks over at Lucy but does not seem to see her. She is like a child herself, but her face is so tired of life that she looks as if she will simply fade to nothing, as if her cells have truly stopped working, as if they are simply drawing her to a close. The gas fire in the corner weeps. It is so cold here among the tiles and damp cardboard. Now the woman strips, pulls up her sweater, shirt, T-shirt and two vests. Her flesh is greasy below the greying bra. As she scratches her stomach, tiny worms of dirt ride out from under her fingers. The woman has a halo of broken short hairs around her head from all the bands and clips she has been wearing. Her breasts bloom wide and flat as she lies back. Lucy rushes at the woman, grabs a couple of bottles and runs. As she clatters down the stairs she hears the woman screaming. Lucy walks quickly and quietly. There is no sign of the men. On the way out she fords a stream of chickens being driven through the centre. She pulls the bottles out and looks at them furtively, ecstatically. Maybe these will cure Reg's women.

Suddenly she hears a voice intone:

"Love is only clouds in a sky of power

I find love when I draw in water, or carve the air."

Lucy runs for a while, down corridors and through yards. She shuts her eyes for a moment and soft blue flames melt her from inside. Her skin becomes a crust for a soul swathed in magma. She walks along, round and down into something like an auditorium, where a large man is on the stage talking and waving things around. She keeps hearing the word 'addiction'. She crawls under a seat. Later she is herded out by a cleaner. Lucy sleeps on some rubbish bags behind a low wall. As she lies tucked between bags, relieved to have found one stuffed with rags or paper towels, a man and a woman stagger outside, drunk, and fuck against the wall. There are crushed beer cans everywhere, some pierced with pens sticking out of them, and bottles on their sides. All the household devils that caused shudders at home – and here she is among them.

It gets late. Reg paces, waiting for Lucy in the fluorescent cell of her lab and wondering if there's any truth in what those guys were saying. She is starting to worry. There is no noise from the flat above. At midnight she turns on the television. A gap-toothed man in a slashed green suit is being addressed by a woman in a pink and blue hacking jacket and silver-grey lederhosen.

… *"The end of ignorance! Nettie, what do you think of that?"*

"Well, it certainly could be, Andy! No more surprises, no more making whoopee either, 'cos you'll be able to tell instantly where little Ali's blue eyes came from, or little Sally's oddly frizzy hair—"

"No, no, Nettie, that's DNA testing, they've been able to do that for years! This is something much better, much bigger. They'll be able to make a map of the entire human body—"

"Complete with service stations! Let's hope the tea's a bit cheaper!"

"Let's not waste the viewers' time sweetheart. They'll be able to tell exactly which genes for which part of the body, behaviour and disease are which."

"And start zapping all those horrible diseases, like plague."

"So, if you discover you've got the gene for something really nasty and degenerative, like Huntington's Chorea, you can forget about having

kids and spend the rest of your life sucking pina coladas."

"You know, recently, women have been committing suicide a lot, and violent crime. I wonder what's wrong with them. It's women with children as well, and women who work with children. I think it's a crying shame. They can't arrest them all. Come on you lot! Where are you hiding?"

"Women have been attacking their own children in increasing numbers. Either that or abandoning them, leaving behind whatever's in the fridge, and disappearing. Tents have even been spotted as far afield as Dartmoor and the Yorkshire Dales!"

"Sounds like they're having a jolly nice time, but what about the kids?"

"They're being put with relatives, as they say."

"Oo-er missis! Don't understand what's going on there."

"Personally, I'd swap the washing up and six blowjobs a week for my own Force 10 and a bit of country air!"

"Causing a bit of a breakdown in schools though — well, it's under control, it just means a lot of men will be teaching the children from now on."

"Interesting! Well Andy, let's hope these sad women manage to sort themselves out in the near future."

"I couldn't agree more, Nettie, I couldn't agree more."…

With trepidation, Reg runs to Jamie's flat. One of the geezers is there, as if waiting for her.

"A woman went bonkers after seeing you. You've done something to that stuff Jamie gave you, aintcha?"

"What are you on about?" Reg knows she must not lose her temper. "Look. So, you got a grant. Great! You know people. Great! But what is that ointment stuff? Did you make it yourselves?" The geezer is implacable.

"You sent a little child to the Market alone to buy needles. We've got it on tape. We're going to report you to the SS."

"Play it to me then. And so what if I did? What a bunch of hypocrites! She works for me, that's all. I look after her. Her home life was worse than you can imagine."

A door is slightly open. Someone is on the phone in an echoing back room. These are big flats. Reg can hardly remember her last visit here.

"Look, let's forget it, OK? If she's all right we can forget the whole thing. Shit, we all want a quiet life don't we? Good joke, yeah?" Reg is sweating slightly. She has not pleaded with anyone for years.

"Too late, Reg."

She stands up and walks towards the door to the room where someone is talking. His murmur echoes.

"…We've got to shut her up so we're gonna take the kid… Yeah, I know, but it's too late now. It's started, and we started it… Yes, but they can't keep up this stupid patter much longer and nor can I, frankly. All that hippy bullshit… You try it then! God, anyone'd think we were fucking artists or something! Ha!… Look, you know the story, it was OK just handing it out at random to get a media snowball going… But then it all went pear-shaped and they're going down like flies… The trains are booked up for years. The roads are jammed. This Regina, she's weird… Stuff happens around her, I don't know. You must have expected something like this would happen and frankly, if you pay peanuts, you get monkeys… We're scientists, not bloody actors!"

She goes through the door. It is just a bathroom. But there is another door which she also goes through. It's a lab, like hers. To her surprise, there is the other geezer. There she was thinking that no-one else but her would build a fucking laboratory in a central London flat. On the walls are maps of the human genome. On the table are a smashed chemical bottle and notes. Reg is furious. How dare they nick her ideas. How fucking dare they? So that's what it's all about.

Reg is a big, strong woman but no match for two men.

Next morning, a bewildered Lucy is walking, her clothes crumpled. She walks about two miles through the early morning grey. She manages a whole road with her eyes shut, even when she passes a little park full of birds. The pavement is slightly uneven so she lifts her feet high like a trained horse. The sun gilds her eyelids, and she sees the red glimmer of her blood pulsing against the true light from above. The smack of a delivery ramp let fall to the ground, the noise like a gunshot, makes her open them for a minute. Her face is flooded with light. She shuts her eyes again.

She comes to a junction and is forced to turn out of the sun. Suddenly it's cold in the half-dark of this pretty street. Radios are beginning to sound; old people, tired of their insomnia, are getting up to put on the tea and think about their futures. Lucy remembers stories she has read about little girls running away from home and finding kind hearts along the paths of independent life.

Lucy hears a noise behind her and scuttles away. She turns another corner, and finds herself in a street of blank shop windows, gilded and barred. The road is silent. An imposing barrier has been put up at each end of it. She stares up into a blank-fronted shop. A large, dark warmth seizes her consciousness from behind.

"Hallo! What are you doing here at this time of the morning, have you run away from home?" The man's voice is rich as caramel cream, old fashioned like his shop but, also like his shop, reinforced with steel.

"Mother run off has she? Father on business?" In Lucy's ears, there is a rumble of a truck waiting to park in a nearby square. The rumble catches a note, perhaps from the old drain cover she is standing on. She feels the lorry's heart as hers, the racing pistons sending their waves roaring through the ground, spreading and spreading. The man is big and friendly, like a big old wardrobe full of pillows in an otherwise empty, echoing house. The man looks swiftly about him, unlocks the door and leads Lucy into the shop. It is dark and the latticed steel blind is thick. But the man does not raise it. He switches off the alarms and puts the kettle on. Dark reddish-brown walls melt the shop's contents into a sheeny patchwork of shapes and figures. However time moves, these artifacts remain the same. Tallboys and cabinets, nests of tables, urns, crocodile skin cigarette boxes and button hooks.

"Look." The man points to an oil painting, thick with varnish, small and low on the wall. It shows a papal scene with two little boys in attendance. The facial expressions are rendered minutely but sharply with swift black brushstrokes, the leer of the Primate contrasting with the blankness of the children.

"The Pope saved little boys from the rabble. Otherwise, they would have begged and been taken and taught to rob and cheat," says the caption.

"Today, this picture is worth ten times what it was worth a week ago, and in a week's time will become unimaginably more precious! The government — do you know who they are? — need these old things because they've got nothing left to sell. Do you understand me?"

Lucy wants some tea and a biscuit. She feels a rush of tiredness in the morning light. She is only little, and looks straight at the painting, not with the crooked pose of an adult. The shop is like her home, although more crammed. Perhaps her father buys things here.

"Has your mother got the problem? Has she run off and left you?"

"Yes."

The man takes her gently by the shoulder, thrusts a Miniroll into her hand, and takes her into the back room where he puts on a tape of *Peter and the Wolf*. He puts one hand on Lucy's body, the other round her neck, and begins to squeeze, delicately.

Lucy suddenly feels the pressure against her rights as acutely as that against her life. She picks up a silver fox's head from the shiny table behind her and thrusts it into the man's face.

The fox head is a door stop. As the man bends Lucy rams it. Afterwards, Lucy runs a hand floppily over her face with the exertion, and trots out into the quiet street, the sunrise glowing in her hair.

There are fewer women about than usual. A boy runs at her. Seeing her face and hands, he stops. There are whispers as she passes the early walkers.

Jamie sits at the foot of a multicoloured structure which looks like an attachment from a giant food processor. He is knackered. They waited all night for Lucy to come out of that fucking church or theatre or whatever it was. And there were people everywhere. Too many people look out for kids in the street these days. Ironic really. Jamie and the others have been signalling to each other on mobiles all night and he's had enough.

Lucy passes him. Jamie beckons to her.

"Your Auntie Regina told me to come and find you. I'm Jamie. She said there was some funny blokes around and not to worry. I'm taking you home. I've got some cold Fishyhugs in my pocket."

Lucy has learnt more in the last few days than in her whole life. However, the lure of cold frozen snacks is nearly too much. She is famished.

She steps on the rainy step and up to the tarnished space egg. Once upon a time it was a fairground ride, the 12 coloured balls whirling around and in and out of each other's trajectories. Now the structure can only turn with regal slowness, the balls swinging gently, their shells splitting and rusting. Inside they are tattered, the curved plastic windows scratched, the white padded ceilings skewbald with patches of cigarette smoke. It is now a café; people get into an egg and suck coffees and teas through lidded beakers, the type taken by children on picnics, while the balls gently grind on. Jamie introduces her to Fipz, another 'mate of Reg's', who is sitting in the egg with a miniature set of bongos hanging around his neck.

"You've got quite a lot of hair, haven't you?" says Lucy. Jamie sniggers in spite of the situation. Hair can be a sign of weakness in a grown man. Prematurely bald men seem to have more energy than the rest, more power. Fipz has a bald patch on the top left hand side of his head from where he has been trying to pull his hair out, but the pain is too much. Fipz was once an in-house mechanic at a laundrette, and sometimes moonlights as a film reviewer. Recently he has been supply teaching geography after three teachers took sudden leave.

Lucy looks at him as the egg bobbles around, showing 360 degrees of small scale wasteland. Lucy's hair tugs against the egg's corroded window rims. There is a muted roar of iron against iron as rusty girders collide. Lucy plays the child now, biting her lip. Lucy puts her hand on Jamie's leg and looks upwards into his eyes, thinking of what she did to the antiques man. The egg swings harder – the ride is ending. They look at Lucy.

"D'you want to come for a little ride?"

"You've just taken me for one," says Lucy. "Where's my Fishyhugs?"

Four of them are sitting in the van. A fat man smiles when he sees Lucy. It is one of the men from the Market.

"Hey, you chased me!"

Lucy is squeezed between them in the back seat. She will not struggle. She will wait. A phone rings. They shoot off. The van bounces over pot-holes. They pass into another borough and the van leaps as it hits the ripples in the road, rocking like a fishing boat.

"I saw Pete Wolf on TV the other day," says Fipz. "He was talking about how clever he was and about how it was really hard to be understood when you were as clever as that and everyone knew who you were. His brother was standing behind him nodding all the time."

"God, he really is an amazing bloke."

"What's so great about him?" asks Lucy.

"He's famous," says Fipz, condescendingly.

"Hur hur! The trouble with God is that he thinks he's Pete Wolf!"

"I think you're all in love with him," says Lucy.

There is an uncomfortable silence.

"I think you should be in love with me. All of you." Lucy is getting squashed.

More silence.

"What's wrong boys, too old for you am I?"

A woman runs down the street.

"I think it's catching now, when you sneeze."

As they move through a school's manor, once barricaded with checkpoints as the children fleeced passers-by for money or drugs, she sees a woman standing frozen, two shopping bags on the ground in front of her. Two little boys are going down the street, tiny, hair long and plaited over their blazers. The woman chews her fingers, the sun catching the tears on her face. Suddenly she picks up the bags and runs, the sharp edges of a large carton jabbing her calves. The children shout something and run after the woman. This time, if at no other, they seem only to want to be friendly. The van waits at a light. The woman rushes up to the van and bangs on the window, Lucy jumps up to get her attention. The woman screams and runs.

"Where are we going?" asks Lucy. "This isn't the way home."

"Don't you worry. We're just going a different way."

They pass another school. It is break-time. The children sit in circles, smiling. Like the last one, this was once the most notorious school in the borough, where the kids fought with every known weapon. Webbed hands were common here, port-wine splashes down faces, bat ears, hare lips sneering; their parents, in protest at the lack of care for all in their vast social bracket, have left these birth defects intact. *Look what you've done to our children*. But over the last year or so there has been a gentleness, like a schoolroom drawing from centuries ago.

Lucy taps her feet against the back of the seat in front. She sees a pair of reflecting sunglasses on the floor. She puts them on.

"Is something fun going to happen now?" she asks.

"We're taking you to our house."

"But I thought we were going to mine."

Silence.

130

"I killed my father yesterday. And a teacher."

Lucy reaches up to stroke Phil's hair. He looks nervous.

"What are you gonna do with the gypsy bitch?"

"Talk later."

"Fuck's sake Jamie, we're gonna have to do it quickly or it's gonna get right out of hand."

"Yuck, yuck, a milk trolley!" Lucy shouts. The trolleys, their engines silenced, play barely audible patterns of soundwaves. It is the cry of the gipsy knife grinder, the ululation that promises a slow rack of ecstasy. A voice sings to Lucy inside, remembering what Reg said about milk. Struggling out of her trapped space, she grabs Phil's arm so that he twists the wheel.

"Kill it, kill it!" the van yaws and charges at the trolley and the man sitting in the cab. Chaos in the van.

"Phil! What are you doing? Stop!" Jamie grabs at Lucy but she scrambles over the seat and steps on Phil's foot.

The trolley-driver has just enough time to run before the van's huge bull nose crumples the trolley into litter and speeds towards the wall. The driver dives and rolls awkwardly into the gutter. The cylinder buckles, falling onto its now flattened side. Bursting from its housing, the faucet clangs against the underside of the van. Milk shoots up in a great spume. The van roars towards the wall. Lucy hurls herself out of the van window before it crashes. She rolls and rolls. The van hits the wall. Lucy runs without thinking, before the pain can kick in.

Reg comes round. The geezer is snoozing in the corner. Her breasts are exposed. For that, she is angry. She hurls herself out of the chair, her twisted arm burning. He jumps up. Reg feels nauseous and retches, demanding, "What have you done with Lucy?"

The man is fumbling for his mobile. He makes a call. Obviously, there is no answer. He nods at the other man. There is a movement behind Reg and the other bloke pulls her down. So he was perving her as well, while she was out.

Reg screams and screams. The geezer laughs. Smelling burnt onions, she collapses.

Reg wakes much later, in a sleeping bag, one hundred and fifty miles away.

seven

"SHE'S COMING ROUND. HELLO LOVE!" Women wearing cagoules surround her. A fire crackles. Someone gives her a huge steaming mug of yeast extract and a stale digestive biscuit. There is some mild singing and an unenthusiastic flageolet. Someone starts talking about 'the colours'. Reg opens her eyes.

"There's a friend of yours here." Lou pulls herself up from a filched pallet. The sun comes out briefly and blares through the skinny canopy as they sit. Cagoules give way to sweatshirts.

"The animals. Who's going to feed the animals? What's happening? Where's Lucy?" Reg has dribbled on the folded sweater under her head.

"You've been very lucky," says Lou. "You were left for dead behind some dustbins in a basement, which just happened to be the flat where Jeanette lives, or used to live." Lou nods towards a pale, hungry-looking woman cooking on the fire. "She was just on her way out the door to come here when she found you."

Jeanette looks over at Reg.

"I brought you with me to Silver Camp because I recognised you from somewhere," she says. She goes back to the cooking without another word.

"Sounds like more than luck," murmurs Reg. Or less, she thinks, dodging the drips from the trees above that spit on the frying tofu.

The English countryside is not at its best in spring. The trees are still skinny and the light is weak, as spring rain falls and beads on buds. The light is grudging through the hard grey trees that surround the flapping encampment below, where terrified women are laid out in ranks, bagged up, masks at the ready, piles of rocks close by. They are in exodus from the city as if from a war zone. Reg, thrown from a car and left for dead, has given them a distraction.

Thirty-five women, dank with the layered sweat of fear, their rank skins running wild after city health regimes, have taken the same buses and trains to the same plains of south western England. They have marched themselves along disused railways, over fences, through wild shrubs, to a wood which they have made their home.

Their camp fire is feeble, glowing green and mauve from the glossy magazines they burn, dropping them at arm's length onto hissing piles of twigs. The women sit; in their empathy, the truest most of them have ever felt, they form circles and talk. But soon they have neither drink nor cigarettes left; they need something else. They discreetly find out if Reg is carrying anything.

The dwellings multiply daily. At the edge of every green space is barbed wire or a lattice with some humming plastic bolus warning the walker to stay back. Young cattle buck and rear with hormones. Farmers bark warnings from a distance as their dogs shove noses in tufts and scamper. Crops are not to be fondled and idly scattered during walks; there are chemicals in them, concealing genes stretched to their limits within the growing seeds.

Women have never been sure whether they really want to get together in groups. Usually, all they know is that from time to time they get very sick of men; therefore they would appreciate refuge with their own kind. But the good feeling only lasts so long.

"I like yellow!"

"I like blue!"

"Well, actually I look really good in lilac!" Conversations become sad choruses for which there is no response, competing to state one's preferences the loudest, as the day passes away above them. After a while, comes the stage of wishing to criticise each other. Some leave room for each others' power trips while pretending not to; others have punch-ups. Boredom has set in; some of them, treacherously, almost wish a child would appear just to give them something to talk about. There are a lot of these fraught fluorescent homesteads. Yeasts play riotously in them, feasting on additives, playing off against the hormones that rage in the water. Each woman has become a host of extra organisms, a suburb of life.

"The local town hall's doubling as a sleepover annexe. Apparently, you should see the number of kids with iron marks on their shirts!"

"And the smell of burning from kitchens!"

Reg sits against a tree stump in the hiss of the morning fire, weighed by tiredness and the hefty unlocking of her memory. Guilt too, at the knowledge that she has not been able to protect the little girl whose own mother she murdered.

Lou does not look pregnant at all, yet is wearing a hideous smock. That silly nickname they had for 'those bits' when Reg was little. All those hours they spent talking about subjects that an average child of that age, at that time anyway, would barely have comprehended.

Reg fiddles with a tin of beans. A small group of primary school children passes at a far distance, checking traps for their biology project, followed by some older orienteers with brand new compasses and anoraks. A few women shout at them to stay back. A couple of bottles are tossed cursorily at them, clinking into the trees. A van toils up to the clearing on the hill.

"Who's that?" asks Reg.

"Who, Rick the Van? He's a local GP with his eye on the main chance, he is."

"Yeah. He got bored of verrucas and arthritic hips, pooled his samples and set up a mobile clinic, supposedly 'for us'."

"No-one wants his drugs. He's tried everything, even recruiting his wife to do the touting with a clipboard, dressed in a uniform with sensible shoes."

Later that day, Rick will come back to find the vehicle entirely smashed, just the frame left, its puny sides buckled, as if a great hand has reached down out of the sky and leant on it.

Only a few tent pegs remain of the teams of counsellors who were flown in and flown out again, equally swiftly. Aborted foetuses are found in streams, wrapped in bins, in hollows of trees. Apparently, the pre-baby makes excellent compost. One female practitioner has become, within a short space of time, highly regarded in the world of market gardening.

Radios chatter over spitting camp fires. The media appear desultorily. Chapped fingers in half gloves grip mugs of broth. The women listen to themselves talked about. Reg sits in her tent and listens to the squeaking of the neoprene. The rhythm starts her mind as she sits out the pain in her side and head.

Regina spent the first few years of her life sleeping on her parents' sofa, a refugee in her own family, having been volunteered at birth to give up her bedroom to some invisible grandparents. She knew no doors between herself and others, no curtain. This taught her to mark out a very special place in herself for everything that was hers. She would paint tiny squirls on the same piece of secret paper until it sagged and disintegrated with the weight of colour. At the time she was still too young to be aware of what might be faulty in her physiognomy, despite the court case and accompanying publicity.

Church should have helped, as her mother repeatedly hinted it would. Mary's heart held one drop of blood for everybody, one dark cell to hide your thoughts in, each person carrying it blotted on paper for their long, lonely journeys. But church seemed the same as the communists and fascists she had read about. Reg was not interested in sitting in a row looking upwards. This was just another bottle of spirits with a grander label, with the horse-brass gleam indulging the people's votary desperation.

As a child, Reg watched her mother cook, clean and cook again. She wiped the sign of the cross on each loaf before she cut it. All that in an empty cell with nothing in it but a bed. Visiting days became pointless, and one day Reg fucked off out of there. As she travelled, she offered herself physically where mere charm was insufficient, performing cold, simple acts which she hoped she would never have to do again. She had the address of a hostel in South West London, where she found a two room space with four people living in it. On the noticeboard in the hostel was a sign, handwritten in round, bubbly script, an offer of work making pretty things in return for money.

At a very young age Regina had to negotiate, Houdini-like, the taut, multiplying trip-wires of her mother's mind. In order not to become insane, Reg had begun life doing such deals with herself as to make those struck with others in later life seem simplistic in comparison. Entering the city, Reg was amazed by the people she encountered, among whom deals were to be avoided, where tacitness was so utter that the air between people hung thick with the unsaid. Albion had become Albino; these pale, tacit people had something missing from their psyches. And here they all are again, avoiding, bodyswerving the truth that is screaming at them. Someone puts the radio on.

...A van crashed in North London this morning, killing all the passengers and injuring a milk-trolley driver. Among the dead were James Oake and Philip Jackson, junior geneticists at the Royal National Laboratories. The others have not been named. Lawrence Mulcahy reports.

"The milk-trolley driver was the only one who saw the incident. He said the van seemed to veer off the road and go straight for him. There is one other person who can help the police with their enquiries. Apparently a little girl was seen running away from the scene of the accident. Police are appealing for her to come forward"...

In a Lowestoft sweet shop at 4.05 that afternoon, Mrs Jackie Twinn, who works there part-time, knocks five jars of Pineapple Chunks, Mouth Orbs and Liquorice Benders on the floor as she tries to escape from a group of schoolchildren. A Coventry woman, Sarah Thorpe, is charged with disturbing the peace and malicious damage when she smashes her way out of the back of a bus, using only a foldable umbrella, after the bus stops outside a school.

In the village of Bridport, Dorset, on the road to Dorchester, Jenny Marles, 38, lashes out at her nephew Tom, ten, with a rake, gouging three bloody welts in his face before he can drop the cheesecake he is giving her and run. He is found sitting in a gigantic tractor furrow, rubbing the cold mud on his face. Police thought she mistook him for an intruder. In Oldham, Liz Parsons, some-time hooker turned drug counsellor, hangs herself when she remembers she has offered to take her sister's children for the week while she goes on holiday to Gran Canaria. Her body turns in the falling winter light, headlamps strobing into her ground floor flat.

Lady Zita Chlorie, a patron of the Revival Foundation for Young People's Education and mother of four, finds herself unable to steer her car on the way to collect them from the Imperial Day School and rams it into a lamp-post, rendering her without sight, hearing or speech for the foreseeable future.

Catherine Salterton, who has a child by Pete Wolf but has long since left that scene – he has forgotten both their names – to live in a top floor in Chepstow Road, West London, catches sight of little Polly, five, on the stairs, eating apple after apple in the true spirit of her father and tossing the cores into a tall narrow glass vase in the corner of the landing, calling it 'Art'. She grips herself with her arms and screams. Polly is used to this and carries on playing. Her mother's screams stop abruptly when she jumps out onto the lawn below. But even the sweet grass is not enough to break her fall. It only disperses the blood that comes from her cracked form.

Catherine's sister Bella sits motionless with horror as her own children eagerly consume the medication she has laid out on the table ready for weighing. She cannot move to stop them, only hide her face while remaining fixed to the spot. They grimace at the taste, which takes time to appear through the ice-cream they have been eating. Bella crawls across the kitchen and sits there, sobbing with terror, wondering who made these small beings with their watching and their needs, their sapping of her body. She wishes her womb is an acid bath, her vagina bristling with thallium-tipped steel. Even as she lies on the floor, she feels herself falling, falling through a waste-water pipe of her own sweat and fluids. She tears at her chest and skin to stop the beating of her heart, like the parachutist who cannot find the string, scraping back to the bone. She bleeds to death, after a long while, as the children paddle slower and slower rings into the carpet.

A canny publican smells something in the air that circulates in his Sussex establishment. His original sign read, "Only very well-behaved children tolerated in the garden." He takes it down and has it repainted. It now reads, "No children on premises – at any time." He likes its delicate crossover between a statement and an order. Scarved women, wearing glasses, scurry from car to door and sit, shaking at his tables. More men come in as a result.

Father Larry Smythe, of Walworth, finds himself in charge of a children's community when desperate working fathers leave their young with him while they look for their wives or persuade them to come out of the garden shed. Father Larry likes children a lot.

Juggernauts come and go, charging the highways like sperm.

Lucy sits outside the building where, ostensibly, she still lives. No-one passes her on this side of the pavement. Darkness falls. Suddenly, out of nowhere come two girls, her age, with shaved heads, one Asian, one white.

"What you doing?"

"Nuffin," says Lucy, "my parents are dead."

"I'm Kerri an' this is Alia. Wanna come with us? We've got food an stuff." Lucy jumps down. She can see them seeing her for what she seems to be. A bit uptight. Only now can she truly see through others' eyes. They don't know what she did two days ago. They are a little bit too sugary-friendly, like Francestina. As soon as they are some way down a path between buildings they turn and push her against the wall. The white girl grips her wrists, the Asian stares her in the eyes.

"You're with us now."

"I thought you weren't gonna ask," says Lucy.

"You cheekin' me?" The girl's eyes are huge, black with orange-white splinters from the streetlight.

"If we can get into the house, there's food there." Lucy knows not to smile too much now. People don't like it. They see it as a sign of submission they can't handle, or an even more intolerable knowingness. But she can tell these two haven't been around for too long.

They march her to a rickety door and down some steps. Four other girls are sitting smoking, none over ten years old.

"What d'you reckon?" said the white girl. They all stand and come right up close to Lucy.

"Looks a bit wet to me."

"There's a house we can get into."

"Ooh, mummy 'n' daddy've got a *house!*"

"It's a flat with stairs in it."

Lucy knows not to say 'actually'. There is a silence, a bit theatrical.

"You ever knocked down a kid?"

There is a general snigger.

"No. But I stabbed my dad in the leg and burnt a woman teacher. A French one. And then this woman I know killed my mum and I was in a van where all these men died who were kidnapping me—"

There is a chorus of laughter.

"Yeah yeah!"

"So what did he do when yer stabbed him, yer dad, give you the needle back and send you up to bed without yer tea?" More guffaws.

"No. He died."

Sometimes truth has a natural authority. They sit down on the damp floor and talk among themselves leaving Lucy sitting, very obviously on her own, on the bottom step.

"They've got me bro on the lacto. Me mum gets it from 'er sister who's a teacher and makes him drink it at home as well as school. It's disgustin'. He told me yesterday."

"You talked to him?!"

"He'd never rat."

They sit for what seems like hours smoking dog-ends and damp, skinny spliffs. From what Lucy can understand, they've all been in the gang for an average of three months. They fight with other kids, but have not done anything worse than steal and survive. Lucy, cold and bored, is making plans.

"Well, if you lot aren't gonna initiate me, I'm gonna try an' get into my parents' place. Anyone coming?"

There is a murmur.

"Wot's 'inishiate'?"

Lucy pauses in herself.

"You know, share blood an' stuff."

"Blood?! Where've you bein idin'?"

They all begin to chant at her.

"HIV, Hepatitis D, E, F an' C, an' not forgettin' – TB!"

Another class she must've missed.

" 'Mon then."

Lucy turns with authority and runs up the steps. There is a mumble down below. She waits two beats before walking quickly and quietly back up the passage.

Reg sits up in her tent. Lou rambles feverishly.

"You know Reg, I was in a bus queue the other day, and this woman was being really rude, and she just kept looking at me as if I was dirt, and you know I thought to myself, 'It's all about her, it's nothing to do with me you know'. I couldn't work out why people are like that, because when I step out into the street I think of everyone as a wonderful human being. I love life. Someone said later that I had pushed in front of her and she had a white stick, but people can be so envious – it's in us all!"

"What a bitch!" Reg murmurs. She is dying to get away. But she is so bruised, so tired, only her mind can go back to the lab.

"Or maybe she was just a kind, loving human being!" Lou remonstrates. Some people can be so tiresome. That cheeky way of waiting till you've given your opinion on something and then deliberately disagreeing with it to make themselves sound pert and clever. It has to be said, Lou still does not look particularly pregnant.

"I can feel it growing inside me, Reggie! It's so exciting that I can provide life to something!" Reg peers out into the day as Lou flutters. Her eyes twitch with mauve fire.

"How does, er, Johnny feel about your situation?"

"Oh, fine! Absolutely fine! Since he feels such compassion for all living beings, he feels joy for me all the time!" There is a pause.

A pigeon roars. Lou cracks open a tin of potatoes. There is so much Reg wants to ask her. There is a courtroom in her mind's eye, and Lou standing as if with a sword.

142

Reg thinks of herself tiny, with all the power of the law supporting her, the fact that she was still alive supporting her, while doctors pinned her back and peered, wheeled her under lasers, rubbing her with greased probes and pointing at screens. As people shouted, her mother sat in her room clutching at the cables which bound her to the world with hooks, which no-one else could see, tearing at her skin as she jerked them.

Suddenly, the pain seems to leave her and Lou smiles smugly, condescendingly at Reg, in a quick way, like Niki did.

"Reggie! Did you ever go and see a therapist after everything? You know, a child psychologist?"

There was too much to do with Reg's mother to leave any time for Reg. She had not been to see anyone, preferring the light that seemed to follow her around.

"No, never." There is a pause.

"He's coming!"

"Who is?"

"Johnny, silly! He's bringing the Positive Roadshow here! You know, Reggie, I think it would be really good for both of us if you came to one of our little sessions. It might help you. There'll be men there, too!"

"I've got to find Lucy. I've got to finish my work."

"Reggie, all this art nonsense. When you're better, why don't you adopt a child? It might make you feel whole again."

In the early evening, a convoy of trucks arrives, one carrying a reconstruction village hall made of canvas which is winched to the ground. Assistants hurry around, inspecting the trees and bushes as if they are buying them. The few men have all come in very small cars.

Lou wheels Reg, heavily swaddled, through the front flaps of the tent, and shoves her forward. Reg snarls under her breath. Having been relieved of a tenner on her way in, she finds herself at the back of a crescent of seats, all occupied. Lou, lost to Reg as soon as she enters the hall, rushes to a reserved seat on the front row.

Reg peers around. The audience is the cast of characters she might have expected at any guru meeting: the fresh-faced and desperate public school man; the lively but sad lady in her fifties, badly bleached hair on top of growing out pink henna with co-ordinating pink clothes, even down to the ankle socks; well-off arty types, fresh from some other self-help meeting, who will repeat the guru's maxims ad nauseam at each other's dinner parties. Then there are the truly helpless, those obviously suffering from awful diseases that ravage the skin, hair and mind, who need so much more than anyone in the room is capable of giving.

Suddenly the lights go down and a figure in a wheelchair rolls silently over a ramp, coming to a halt in front of them. When the spotlight comes on Reg is transfixed with horror, and love.

It's Joe Lehman! Or Johnny the Layman, as he is now known, the one who got her thrown out of college. The bright light on his face causes her eyes to stream. Soon after Reg left, he had an accident and was confined to a wheelchair. That's what the press said, anyway. At the time, Reg rejoiced in her own mental powers, even as she burnt her books. Someone next to Reg thinks she is crying and touches her arm. She shudders with pain from the bruises.

Johnny waves to the audience. Instantly they shut up.

"Hi! Welcome to Positively *Charged!* I've *changed* today! I've *moved on.* How about you?" His voice is clear and cajoling, slightly higher than you might expect.

Reg remembers reading about Joe, adulatory profiles and, as he became more established, half-hearted exposés. He always had interviewers eating out of his hand. He already had an office when Regina was still seeing him, for some charity campaign he'd cooked up. A student with his own office!

Joe ran things. Joe ran people. When he was at his work, there would be a knock at the door. An impressionable student manager would come in and report that two of the staff were fighting. Without looking up, Joe would throw him the key to his cupboard and say to try the hardware first. The manager would pull out two cartoon-size hammers with soft rubber ends. Taking them over to the fighting pair, he'd send them into a spare room to thrash it out. Larger scale bad atmospheres were solved with paint guns. Those peace-making exercises for his part-time staff gained him a reputation for fairness.

In fact, the disputes were nearly always engendered by Joe in the first place. He discreetly removed a paper from a file, secretly cancelled other peoples' meetings or, his favourite, promoted the least deserving of two people who had to work together. New helpers, of which there were very many to type and file for him, were welcomed by an unpleasant ritual of blood taking and fingerprinting. No-one was sure if it was entirely legal, but they were rushed through it barely having taken their coats off.

Like many leaders, Joe existed mainly in his employees' imagination; clearly, like all gurus, Johnny now exists almost entirely in his flock's. As with many manifestations of personal power, his was actually highly comical, but the structure he devised became so quickly established that none dared mock the façade. He sought out weaknesses and picked at them till they were raw as the day they were engendered. To compensate for this state of unease – Reg remembered having her doubts about him even before what happened – he discreetly spread among his workers the age-old rumour that a particular set of keystrokes, in this case shift-control-left bracket, would "bring the whole fucking thing down." In other words, it would erase every file and software program in the system. Of course, no-one ever dared to try it, but they all talked of doing so, quietly, over coffee or in the pub after work. As a staff comforter this technique has no equal, and costs nothing.

He has strong arms and shoulders which he flexes when not wearing a shirt. When Reg knew him, Joe loved to taunt female employees with his power, knowing they condoned his behaviour because they were liberal, at least in speech, whilst strict on themselves. A certain kind of woman loved to work for him. They still do, judging by the number of solicitous creatures flapping around at the beginning of the session. Solid, middle-aged, dowdy, large glasses; hard working, had a bit of a career, got a bit tired of it, as women do, and found it easier to be resolute upholders of the department ethic with their helplessly twee workstations. However swiftly ergonomic the office furniture, anyone trying to personalise their space creates a shrine to banality and homeliness: the pathetic gonks; the ancient newspaper clippings with their name on; miniature bullfight posters, also personally identified; the barrage of weakly hostile admonitions word-processed and stuck up on the wall. "Lack of planning on your part does not constitute an emergency on my part."

Reg read how Joe's employees could never stand the sound of his wheelchair, the hiss of no-sound as it kissed the ground. He had it built tall and broad, with great doric legs of metal supporting the full-tyred wheels. Its arms contained pop-up screens and pill dispensers. The chair's height allowed him to look down comfortably at those sitting, while still being slightly shorter than them when they stood up to argue with him, making him appear vulnerable.

After his mysterious accident, Joe was obsessed with electronics but even more with power. He enrolled himself in every experimental programme he could get into to learn about the future, from advanced biofeedback onwards. He read every available study on the subject; when it went beyond a matter of the unicorn attachment and began to explore the role of brain function, he was away. He learned to drive a car using first nods then eye movements, then impulses he could barely comprehend. Joe won awards for his dedication to research.

Once free of bureaucratic constraints, he started a campaign to attack large companies, threatening them with exposure of their many pricing discrepancies until they had sets of ramps and lifts put in for disabled employees. This gained Joe grass-roots support. As did his threat to expose the secret activities of one large supermarket chain, only withdrawn when they agreed to run two sets of shelves, high and low. Finally the government saw his point and funded his charity action group, which soon became an 'organisation'. Stannah stairlifts became the cutting edge of political trendiness, as Joe vowed, "One in every home in the next two years." Stairlifts changed their look from Parker Knoll on runners to a whole variety of designs: black leather; grey velvet; chintz; wave movement and cable car-style. They rewarded him greatly when even the fully-abled began ordering them. His organisation became a 'department' and he became more and more distanced from his old companions. Gradually, imperceptibly, his mind turned a corner, taking his attitudes with them. He hadn't got where he was by having it easy. And then Joe disappeared. Now, he is a guru.

Emotionally, Joe took Reg to the cleaners. The memory is unbearable. He tapped into her brain, but she did not realise until it was too late. He grassed her up to the authorities about what she was doing, although she could never prove it.

Even then all she could think of was the fucking, the bleakly brilliant screws they had, always under fluorescent light. She made herself there for the taking. With Joe, it was so easy not to be in control. He would snap his fingers if no-one was around, or signal by singing a tune if they were at a party. He would plough into her like a car smash on the motorway played again and again, faster and faster, until her heart and mind were blurred by his power.

Joe had loved her once, she was sure, as he dragged her up the stairs in a neck-lock, threw her on the bed, made her jerk him with a smooth hand and had her soft lips pinch and smother wetly at his glans while his hand forked her hair. They made shapes together; she buckled herself onto him by the light of a street-lamp through thin curtains. They hinged and flexed until they were half dead with pleasure.

After Joe, she did not fuck anyone more than once for ten years.

Johnny's voice is deeper, darker. "There's always time for a change! You may be hurrying to work, no time to eat, no time to tie your shoes, but there's always time for a change!"

147

Reg feels charged with fear, even as she sits unnoticed, charged like a battery, charged like a defendant under the accusing eye of her past. What did she not let this man do to her?

"Always time for a bit of a change!" calls the audience. A woman starts talking about some really ugly scaffolding on the house opposite her bedroom window. Johnny cuts her short.

"Are you so much better looking or useful than that scaffolding, Petra? Don't you think you were talking about yourself when you had such a negative thought?" The woman looks angry, clearly not used to this kind of treatment, then confused, then pacified.

"So who's got a story for me today?" Johnny asks.

"Me, me, me!" yells a woman, who Reg recognises as an ex-breakfast television presenter. "Hello everyone! I went to Nathan's Bar & Grill the other day and had lunch with Hitler, the Devil and Robert Maxwell!" There is a gasp of admiration tinged with sympathy.

"Ooh, how was that ?"

"Lovely. Absolutely lovely. And then I told the story to my friend and she said, 'I don't believe you'. I mean, what does it take to persuade these people? I said, 'It was lovely' and she said, 'But I mean, take the Devil, for instance, surely he must have been a *bit weird!*' " There is laughter.

"That's the spirit, Mary. Don't let people bring you down. If you had a good time with those guys, then you had a good time. Your friend was just jealous. You see, when you have something, other people sometimes feel inadequate. But the thing is, good fortune is there for us all. You just have to reach out and take it. OK, who's next?"

The pink lady speaks up.

"You know, Johnny, what I just wanted to say was this. We, we are the creative ones. No-one else really understands this. Every day, after I've done an hour at my easel, I go out into the street and just stand there, all day, looking at the colours. The colours! Yellow makes me feel very intense at the moment. Then I go home again. Every evening I look out of the window and say to myself, I am in my life, I am in my life, I am in my life!"

A man with a straggly ponytail speaks up, "Er, noticeboard everyone! The other day I was looking for a flat. The person from the letting agency told me a rent for this place I'd just looked at. He got up to do something and I noticed that he'd told me a higher figure than what was written on the paper. I said to him, 'Why did you do that – are you going to give the extra to charity?'" There is applause.

"Anyway, does anyone know of a flat going in North West London, one bedroom, preferably south facing?" Various people speak up and pass phone numbers to the man. Some pat him on the back and shake his hand. Johnny speaks.

"You see, if that letting agent had taken the extra money and given it away he would have got something back. He could *change* himself—"

"Always time for a change!" shouts the crowd, Lou particularly loudly. The guru talks for ten minutes on the importance of giving and taking, then asks if anyone has any more to say. A man speaks.

"My girlfriend committed suicide 12 years ago because we were different religions. Now, I still just can't seem to have relationships." Silence falls. After several seconds deliberation, Johnny speaks.

"Well, er, you must, er, have relationships," says Johnny. Something whirrs in his wheelchair. The silence continues. Someone passes round a party hedgehog, a melon with little cubes of tofu and quail's eggs on the sticks. A fire spits outside. He has not mentioned, yet, why there are several thousand runaway child-phobic women camping in the middle of Wiltshire, nor how he can help them.

"My brother died last year," a small woman in a navy blue suit whispers to Reg, who is drumming her fingers on the arm of the chair, one shoulder further forward than the other as if ready to charge.

"I'm sorry," says Reg.

"Oh, it's not your fault," the woman replies, smugly, patting Reg on the hand.

"Of course it's not my bloody fault!" Reg hisses, "How could I be in any way responsible for her death?" She wheels herself out, catching her oversized coat on chairs and umbrellas. Outside, the spring night taunts her. Reg feels disgust followed by rage. She flops on a hummock of grass. She hears the word 'donation', and the gravelly voice of Johnny's pet soap star reaffirming her own success. There is a short silence before people start to file out. They mill by the entrance to the hall, gripping each others' arms. Lou, who keeps tucking her hair behind one ear, rushes over to Reg.

"Well, I think I'm ready now. I'd like you to have a look at me tomorrow."

"Erm, I'm not a gynaecologist…" Bats ride the night, their wings whistling.

"I know! I want you to share my joy! I'm going to learn so much about myself!" she coos, as she sashays awkwardly in front of Reg, coquettish like a horrible child. Reg pulls her ear. The world suddenly has no safety rail any more. She is off the promenade, reaching the far end of the Cobb. The way he fucked her, the drugs they took, the laughter.

"So, when's the happy day?"

"That's the point, Reggie, I'm not even on a waiting list. Remember all those drugs I did?"

"Well yes, but childbirth has some priority over sin, doesn't it?"

"Oh, you silly moo! I'm not pregnant! I've got cancer!"

What, rising? wonders Reg. "For God's sake, haven't you had any treatment at all?" She looks in horror at Lou.

"Johnny told me my cancer's good for me. It'll make me a better person. He got the group to do Wiggly Fingers to me for a whole minute. Then we did another 'Anybody Need Anything?' Someone asked if anyone had a BMW they were willing to trade for a fur coat. Oh, and there were some lovely tips on cooking with kumquats."

Reg feels as if she is picking glass out of her face.

"Cancer's not decay, it's growth!" Lou insists. They talk for hours.

Later, Reg dreams she lays a huge strand of eggs. Jets of white envelop it as she swims away. She wakes to the sound of women sniping at each others' hairstyles, even though, after several weeks living outside, there is very little to distinguish between them.

The next day the group is united again, by an event caused partly by the increasing number of high security lorries that roar to and fro down the tiny country road running half a mile or so from the camp. Over the rise is an old farm building, long and flat, that has been tarted up with red signs and electric fencing. The farmer who owns it – now being paid a rent that is, frankly, stupid – will not be drawn on its new purpose.

Reg joins three of the especially bored women as they go to see the farmer to get chocolate and Lucozade. The days of milk and eggs being purchasable from farms are long gone. They all have to be sent to a plant to be treated; though for what, is never made entirely clear. The farmer has a mate who spots stray boxes outside village groceries, leaving behind the grey onions and scorched-looking carrots. Vegetables don't seem to feature much on this farm either.

They all sit on his front step, have a cigarette in the wind and haggle over a carton of Snickers. While the farmer is fetching it, a huge lorry appears and begins going down the lane to a large, flat-roofed building known locally as the Shed. Jumping up, the women run down the hill after it, for something to do. Reg gets the Snickers and walks after them. She must leave soon to find Lucy. All the other women want is something to protest about, or at least talk about. They are so eager to see what is in the lorry that they do not notice the silent scene happening in the field in front of them. They rush on, before coming to a terrified halt.

Before them, an adult in a red anorak, bright against the field, squats on one knee, leaning over a child, thin and green-looking, whose face is turned at an odd angle towards the sky, and in whose frail lap lies a tiny lamb, shaded dark with jet black hooves. There is, between sight and screams, a minuscule sliver of time when the women see the blind, incurable orphan child on the last special day out of her life, with the social worker from the hospice, sitting on the damp grass, the moisture soaking into her jeans. It doesn't matter because she is going to die soon anyway. The sleepy runt lamb does not have long for this world either, and feels no need to struggle. That is, until the gang of women rush up like bullocks, screech and rush away again. Reg sees the social worker fall back. The lamb leaps to its feet; with its last energy, it staggers away, tripping on the tussocks of grass. The little girl just sits there, motionless.

eight

REG BENDS AND GRIPS AT INVISIBLE FENCE POSTS. There is a sound of hooves kicking up the ground behind her, and a hot snorting at her neck. She lowers her body to take the creature's full weight, a huge baton of flesh nudged up against her vagina. Miraculously it slides into her, right in, 20 inches or more of curved shaft, mining her. She breaks her breathing quickly and rides out the sensation, all her body organs pushed up and out, crowding into her gullet towards the light. The animal thrusts harder. Reg slings herself lower, the animal setting up a discordant scraping bellow. Reg's head is rammed against the fence, her hair tugging. It shoots into her with a scream, handfuls of thick fluid squeezing out of her and dribbling onto the ground. The creature vanishes.

Reg wakes to the sound of a horse neighing in a field half a mile away. She aches.

Another group of women has arrived, looking stilted and tired. Reg walks around. Lou's news has made her angry. Even more angry with Johnny for that, than for what he did to her. She leans on a gate, the lichen brushing onto her sleeves. Someone clears their throat behind her. She turns. The person standing there does not look very friendly, as if she thinks Reg has taken something from her. Reg used to get this when she regularly wore a jewel-encrusted djellabah, but not now, surely, when she is wearing a borrowed heap of brown sweaters and tracksuit bottoms.

"Well, if it isn't our own Florence Nightingale. Regina Voss, who knows everything!" It's Lara, the delicately scornful chief nurse of the hospital where Reg used to do part-time numerological counselling. She used a filthy, worn keyboard with grimy patches under the most popular letters. Reg would take the ten dirtiest, translate them into numbers and tell the future with the result.

Once Lara, costing herself a fortune in pride, came to Reg with a problem. Something like an affair, an intensity, developed between them. From the start they both knew that Lara resented her own dedication far more than Reg's freedom of existence. Lara believed in healing, curing, saving, helping others. She hated herself for it. Now, Reg sees Lara and the past comes closer, all over again.

Back then, Lara had searched everywhere for an upturn in her spirit, a broad-palmed religion. She tried them all; moved across from Buddhism to lunacy and back again. She could not find one belief-station that could explain to her how not to believe, but simply to live; how to obey the yearning of the heart.

Now, Lara has hit her thirtieth birthday and met the older, darker Reg with her voice like rotting fruit and petrol, with her reputation. How could Lara not look back on her own life and see nothing but a trite labyrinth of process, exam, slight elevation, chocolate medal, next bend in the corridor, all under a dull strobe of curtains opening and closing. Lara had hunkered down by the small, smelly, whistling camp fire in herself, thinking she could never change.

Reg and Lara brush cheeks and fingers, Lara's hostility vanishing like a snowflake. The smell of the hospital comes back to Reg; the damp ceiling of the above-ground catacomb, ancient flecked grey walls with a once crimson dado rail, the place echoing with entreaties, creaking bed bases and the slice-slice of corroded daisy-wheel printers. Reg sees Lara is in too much of a hurry for pride.

"Reg, we've just arrived. We need your help."

A newcomer is sick. They asked if Johnny's roadshow could stay as a shelter, but it could not. The woman is lying in a bash of badly stitched tarpaulin, her feet rubbing the ground like a stubborn animal's. There is a pool of yellowish shit streaked with blood, hidden mostly by her skirt which has dragged it around in stiff woollen folds. It is an amoeba, probably, but the woman sobs and crawls, finally pulling her skirt aside.

A huge worm, tapered like a giant rat's tail, lies in the pool, tipping slightly at the end. Reg has never actually seen one of these before. The poverty worm, a columnist called it. The clumsy, dated, PC name has stuck. This worm lives on extra nutrition, all the hormones, vitamins and supplements that get stuffed into meat, chicken and vegetables. What ultimately causes it to mutate out of nowhere are the pills, bought from the sawdust-floored shops, that people think they are keeping themselves alive with. Mineral water, cause of a generation of children's rotten teeth because of fear and snobbery towards tap water, is too weak to kill it. There is a silence. What is Reg expected to do now? Rub Vick on it? She pats her pockets and feels a tiny tin. All this time she has been carrying some of that fucking ointment. Pulling it out, she rubs it along the worm's length. It arches its body into a sensuous curve and pulls out of the woman with a loud suck. It lies on its back, twining its tail with increasing violence. Tighter and tighter it winds; whether with agony or pleasure is impossible to tell. It winds and winds until it is a Gordian ball of tightly locked matter, then falls still. It has entirely merged with itself.

"It's an omen," someone says.

If only Reg's mother could have been cured like that. If only the gimlet of horror in her mind could have been transformed into something living. Her mother, wrapped in her own invisible worm, looking up at Reg would say, "It's like there's a winch, a giant winch inside my head, with every nerve, vein and artery wrapped around it. There's a giant handle against my skull; people are queuing up to turn it until every string in me yanks and yanks. It yanks, Regina. Why do English people always queue?"

Her incantatory murmurs told of a world about to end. Her world only, Reg always thought. But now she is not so sure.

People look at Reg in awe as the woman calms down.

"Reg, you can help Lou, too. Yes you can! She still doesn't believe she's ill. Johnny told her she wasn't—"

"—And then someone nicked her codeine. It took us ages to get it." A pleading chorus. Reg cannot stand this. But there is nowhere to run. Green nature will see to it that she is seen. Rage builds in her.

Lou is lying down, looking entranced through her pain, sweating.

"Everything's so lovely!"

"Lou!" shouts Reg, "You're not in recovery, you've got cancer!"

Reg picks Lou up as gently as she can, still not knowing where her cancer is, and takes her to the trestle table in the little copse. Someone runs behind her with blankets.

"This is just us two, OK?"

She lies Lou on the table.

"Lou, Johnny the Layman is a fraud!"

"No, he's not! And anyway it's in us all!"

"No, it's *not* in us all! *You're* not a fraud, *I'm* not a—" At this point Reg feels a twinge of guilt. "And neither are them over there!"

Reg dabs a tiny amount of the ointment on Lou's stomach. It doesn't affect her at first. The interrogation continues for several hours. Lou is not even allowed to go to the toilet.

"Reggie, Reggie, the world's going to end soon, I know."

"Yeah, right,"

"Reggie, my cancer comes from my family. All the women got it because they overstretched themselves. My mother was a doctor, her mother was an activist, but they were always so unhappy. It's so much easier for a woman just to be married. And now I'm the same. A lawyer punished for my ambitions, punished for enjoying life at the same time—"

"Cobblers!" shouts Reg. "Don't tell me, your cancer is God punishing you for trying to be something you're not?"

That old chestnut, used to undermine women since the beginning of time. Lou shakes her head. She clutches the hem of her sweater. There is a silence.

"Reggie, you do know what it was all about, don't you?"

"What was all about?"

"The court case. I mean they did tell you what was wrong?"

"It was some gynie thing to do with how I was born."

"Didn't they tell you?" Lou lies back and gasps with pain, but still beatific.

"Look, Reggie, you know you can never – ha! – have children?"

"I must say, I haven't really thought about it."

"Liar, Reggie. Do you realise that all the weird medication they gave your mother, all the stuff they tested on her, even before you were conceived, did something to you?"

"What?"

"Reggie, you were born without a womb. We had to keep it all secret because some women's pressure group people wanted to expose it, then some other people said the drug would be really good for eugenics. Well, obviously they didn't call it that at the time. They started testing again but I don't know what happened next because I was too busy with my career. We thought someday someone was going to find you and use you for tests or something. So it was all kept quiet. My guilt hasn't helped me, I know—"

So that was the pain inside that Reg always felt. A phantom. The doctors long ago explained that she could expect something inside her to bunch like a fist, or waft and billow from pain to pleasure and back.

Once, Reg might have been aborted. For a few years, her mother was allowed to roam free in the community, whatever that was. They thought it would be better for her than echoing incarceration in a urinous, linoed prison. But the streets were worse. Who was it that slipped inside Reg's mother? A policeman? Or the mayor, his chain swinging cold against her back after belching his way through a speech at some Rotarian saturnalia? Pregnancy had not helped Reg's mother, who instantly forgot the sex, only becoming aware of the pregnancy when Regina started to show.

Lou writhes and sweats. Reg makes plans in her head. They will campaign together when she is better.

By 4 o'clock in the afternoon, Reg has got Lou to admit that she might not win the lottery the next day if she gives a tenth of what she hopes to win to Johnny. Suddenly she jumps.

"Christ! It's wriggling! Oh my God, I feel fantastic! It's like a blob of honey ricocheting around inside me. Argh!"

"Push!" shouts Reg. "Repeat after me, 'Resistance is not denial and I am responsible for my actions.'"

"'Resistance is not' – but it *is* – OK OK! 'Resistance is not denial and I am responsible for my actions.'" Lou gives an orgasmic shriek, arches her back, and out from under her skirt bounces a small blackish blob, which rears up threateningly before tearing off into the undergrowth, making sticky noises as it jumps. They sit back, exhausted.

"God, I feel such a fool," says Lou. The bright and shining mask of self-delusion has melted from her face. She lies back, dying instantly.

Reg does not cry, but walks past the crowd, out of the wood and down the road to the village. As she walks Reg finds a couple of tiny pots of as yet unused ointment in her pocket and takes some. She steals a cream-coloured hatchback with light emerald interior and dark pink metallic detailing which is parked at the roadside. She curses its silly appearance, like a make-up compact on wheels. She drives back to the city.

As Reg reaches the M25, a large brown blanked-out van appears from nowhere and edges up, closer and closer. There is a 'chunk' as it bashes into her. She tries the accelerator, then the brake, before realising that she is being carried along by a force she cannot explain. They travel like this for several minutes, before Reg realises something is happening to the road beneath her. It seems to be directing her, rippling up specially to catch her wheels and drag her onwards. Suddenly she has her own lane, like a Korean leader. She drives until she comes to a town. She walks into a grocers and leans heavily against the doorway. Every foodstuff she can see in front of her is gradually reduced to its constituent parts. She sees a bag of flour and, the next moment, a shimmering sea of corn. She sees bacon on the cold shelf and then a pig in a brown meadow; a bag of rice and then sloshing paddyfields. The woman behind the till, in a blue gingham housecoat, is tired and flattened by her job. She shakes in front of Reg before transforming into a column of jelly that falls to the ground with a clap. Reg thinks she may as well rob the till, but on opening it sees only ore. The till itself begins to reduce. The counter becomes trees, their great trunks barging out of the ground. She backs through the door and leans on the car, ignoring the filthy bloom on it. It begins to soften and yield to her body, the cream metal turning first to mosslike sponge and then to muscle. Reg rolls from side to side in the grasp of this sofa-like creature with huge pink and green pores that flex open and closed independently, as if breathing with hundreds of lungs. Slowly it takes her in its embrace.

Lucy is waiting in her flat when Reg arrives. Music thumps above them. Reg picks her up and hugs her.

Lucy has already moved on, recent memories erased.

"Regina, Regina, my friends saw me on the radio! And there's something else, there's something wrong with the animals."

Without stopping to find out how Lucy got in, Reg rushes to the lab. The creatures are slowed by mucus, their food uneaten.

"You were gone for a week, I didn't know where you were. It's got really weird now, loads of women are going and there's all these boys and men everywhere. And there's these vans going around making announcements. I don't like it. Tell me a story."

"The little house-breaker wants a story!" Reg talks distractedly as she prepares the antibiotics. "OK, you little brat, listen, here's the rest of that story about the apple, remember? One night it was glowing so brightly they all went out into the garden to have a look at it. Nothing happened, so they went back indoors. The years passed and they all died, but the apple remains, because it is totally made of chemicals designed to imitate nature. The moral is, the mechanical bastard always wins."

"Will you mechanise me like you did that baby?" asks Lucy. "You can come and meet my new friends if you want. I've been hiding."

Reg does not reply. She feels herself beginning to weep.

"Can you not do your show now? Couldn't the rats being ill be part of it? But I suppose it's quite a long time till June. They might die before then."

"Yes, I know they might fucking die."

Reg is acid. Lucy looks more knowing. She plays *Blast The Past* more vigorously than Reg thought her capable. Suddenly she asks, "Why does it ask for my id? My User-id? What about my user-ego? What does the machine really want to know? Is the id of me-as-user the same as me-as-me, or does the identity of the user change as he or she uses? Like when the thing changes when it's being observed?"

God knows where all that's coming from. Reg pulls some meat from the fridge and eats it, famished. Lucy is getting fatter, or at least larger. Her eyes and upper lips are creasing like a long term smoker's.

"Reg, I want to see you fuck. Why don't you do that on stage." The little girl's demand has the ugliness of a fly settling on a stale cream cake. But, like the fly, it is not incongruous.

"Well, you can't. I don't want to, for a start."

Lucy shows a halo of white burns on the inside of her wrist.

"What the fuck are those!" Reg sits up, her will to be a therapist returning.

"Part of my initiation ceremony. They didn't have one so I invented one."

"Lucy, for God's sake, my work's ruined! Can't you just shut the fuck up!" shouts Reg.

"Re-eg, I'm still your familiar, aren't I! Oh go on, I am, aren't I?" Lucy picks up the gun and bops it at the screen. "I want to add some stuff to Blast The Past." The screen is slow to give her the image she wants. "Get some more RAM for fuck's sake!"

Reg's eyes go to the hammer on the sideboard, then to Lucy, then back to the hammer again. No, she created this Lucy, too. It's not Lucy's fault.

Lucy takes Reg by the hand and leads her upstairs. Lucy spits, voluminously, to a perfect rhythm like a garden sprinkler, in the faces of everyone present. They do nothing.

"We're going to have some fun with the Steals, aren't we girls!" she shouts.

Reg feels iron in her soul, and in her blood.

She leaves the house and walks. Reg is accosted by people trying to persuade her to become a nurse, teacher, even a surrogate mother. Someone hands her a flyer. She is about to screw it up when she notices the big 'I' on one side.

"The Famous, Permanently Installed, Wolf Brothers!" Pete Wolf is a big name. At least, lots of people talk about him. He courts fame the way most people breathe, although no-one is quite sure what he actually does, or where he gets his money from. Self-promotion has fast edged past talent as a justification for success.

Reg walks half a mile or so to the converted church which was a supermarket before being abandoned and then recaptured by the Wolfs. There are so many ex-churches around the city as to be quite embarrassing. Based loosely on an amphitheatre, the Wolf's venue has a fully operational Intensive Care Unit, banks of monitors, a lounge bar upstairs, and living quarters arranged around the stage, all decorated with a rotating set of brand names. The place is known, informally, as Neuremberg.

A door opens ahead of Reg. An aggressive door-whore with a lilac rinse and a gold shirt glares at her, demanding a fee.

"Help us resolve the Art v Science debate!" the promotional screens demand. Critics complain, on the right because the brothers use drugs and because it is 'not art'; on the left because the Wolfs, as well as being well-off in their own right, have become rich enough to own a huge double fronted house in West London, but are ploughing nothing back into the community, except into entertainment. "The human embodiment of the will to trivia," is how one magazine describes them. "They have tapped into the cult of the vicarious," says another. They live and sleep on and around the stage, some of the time at least. The show has a beginning and an end in that they get up at some point during the day and go to bed later on. Otherwise, the audience observes them by walking around until they have heard everything, then leaves an appropriate donation so the brothers can go and score. Rob controls the business side of things while Pete is the creative one, the self-styled Giant Child, thumping surfaces with a large spoon whenever he needs anything, which is nearly all the time.

Reg sits down next to a dark haired man who introduces himself as Seb Aldiss, the editor of a fashion-science crossover publication. Reg does not usually spend much time with young media types; the combination of cocaine and eagerness with the desperation not to seem eager, soon palls. He chats her up by default, since she is female and looks scene-related, if a little older than average.

"So yeah, my name's Seb Aldiss and I'm an Emotional Neotenist. The guys are sponsoring the magazine." He speaks with a carefully fatigued upper class drawl.

"The point is, people've known for a long time that long-term heavy drug use retards emotional development. Loads of people are walking round with, basically, the hearts and minds of 18 year olds, which is the average age when most people's habits've started to get a proper hold on them—"

"Ah yes," says Reg, "women tend to notice this on dates and comment on it to their friends." Seb laughs wryly.

"Anyway, I've written loads about it in the style press, and then I did some stuff about Pete and Rob, so we got together and decided to set up the magazine. Look, d'you like our mascot. It's a newt! Nature's prime exponent of neoteny!"

Seb becomes excited.

"Bill Burroughs is one of our patron saints!"

"Oh yeah," says Reg. The luminous bourgeois whose image remains forever installed in the third eyes of his fans. "Dead guy, yeah? Surely he's been, er, discredited by now?" she asks.

"Like Shakespeare or Freud, I suppose," spits Seb, Reg's attractiveness forgotten.

"Smack shifts copies, I guess!" laughs Reg. There is an awkward silence.

There is noise from the darkened stage. A man a few seats in front of Reg suddenly speaks up, nervously.

"God, I drank 12 cups of coffee yesterday. It was unbelievable!" The lights go up. Pete Wolf looks up from the stage and gives him a scathing stare.

"I drink twice that on a *normal* day. What kind of coffee was it, anyway?"

"Oh, all kinds, really. I mean I kick start with a Nescafé at home in the morning you know, it's quicker. I move on to Lavazza at work, or Kenco when my assistant's forgotten to get Lavazza, then on to Nescafé in the afternoon, but it's not the same, it really isn't. And when I'm working on a project from home—"

Pete cuts him off with a sneer.

"Rob, what are we doing even breathing the same air as these fucking lightweights? Look mate, what's your name?"

"Er, Simon."

"Look, *Er Simon,* I have my Gaggia on all day. They come and descale it once a week. In fact, and don't tell anyone," this is one of his favourite catchlines, which means everyone has to stop and listen, "but I actually fixed some once!" There is a theatrical gasp.

"You didn't!"

"I certainly did! But it wasn't the same 'cos I couldn't smell it. I tried making a separate pot so's I could smell it while fixing up but, you know, even excess palls occasionally, don't you think? Har har har!" Pete Wolf's voice booms around the vast space. Reg, sensitised, feels a strange breeze pull the hairs on her skin in different directions, like the wind in a wheat field.

When a person becomes famous, their grandness seems to increase exponentially each time you see them. Perhaps it is just because you fancy you have a familiarity with them that increases every time you find yourself in their presence. With Pete Wolf, his grandness increases each time Reg looks away and then back at him. He exudes possibility. His fans lap up his every personal detail, as released in the media, in their desperate attempts to achieve a unique closeness with someone entirely self-invented.

Pete staggers up from the vast ottoman he has been lying on, clutching his head.

"First degree hangover! Oh Christ! I once had to go on telly when I'd had four bottles of wine, five brandies and half a bottle of calvados. It all started to sound like some terrible perversion of that Christmas song, you know, four French hens and stuff. Fuck—"

Rob interrupts, coughing and lighting up, saying encouragingly to Pete, "I'm on my fortieth and it's only 2 o'clock."

There is a resentful squeak from one of the girlfriends who meander sharply in the background. Pete's love-life is so complicated that it has been turned into a board game by a consortium of art students. It is selling like hot cakes. A movie deal is on the horizon.

Reg has met these girlfriend-types before, in her own home, as clients, the trivia of their lives requiring a more patient medium than her to flick out their problems. Most of them would come armed with their own and their targets' star charts, demanding to be shown the likelihood of love. Some, she now realises, must have been talking about Pete. The girlfriends are definitely 'not stupid', although the concept of being 'not stupid' covers a multitude of means of survival in society. They have long realised that it is easier to sleep with well-known men to get on than attempt creative achievement themselves. They pout, frown and stomp their pretty feet at each act of inebriation or infidelity, but take it on the nose, as there is much mileage in being known as a Wolf companion. Whenever Pete collapses or becomes comatose, one or more of them rushes to his prone form and ministers to him, perhaps an enema or cold compress. It is early in today's performance, so Pete is still comparatively sober. He chops out a vast line of cocaine, hoovers it up and starts talking about computers.

"We did it, me and Rob, we did it, we bust the cartel! Remember the days when your PC was out of date within six months; you just had to go and buy another one. Well, we discovered that they put a slow-acting timed-release substance under the keyboard, just like Hunter S Thompson's soaked towel under the accelerator. Wow, what a hero! Anyway, we discovered that they were putting this addictive gas stuff there which would wear off after six months, so you'd start wondering why you wanted the PC in the first place and go off and buy a new one. We told all the consumer pages and got them to put a great big ad in the papers. Now it's fucking brilliant 'cos everyone's got choice, haven't they?" Rob steers him over to a table, where Pete proceeds to eat a succession of peanut butter sandwiches which he then throws up.

"The point is, I'm not like other people. You see, I have a very special mind and my needs are greater and more complex than other people's, basically."

"Have you tried just saying 'no'?" calls a woman from the front row.

"You don't understand, I can't help it, it's in me. I just can't stop."

Reg thinks she could work with this man and wonders, like many women before her, if collusion really could be the better part of valour.

"Tea, now there's a heavy one," interjects Rob, who is still coming to terms with his brother's more successful attention-getting, although he is the vital money-man.

"Tea! Fuck, I just can't leave it alone. Tea is the higher power I am helpless to control, but it's not my fault." With a flourish, he prepares a pipe from a small plastic bottle and a biro, and places a small lump of something in the top.

"That's crack cocaine," Seb whispers to Reg.

"Oooh really? Not 'crack' then? So let me get this right," she whispers, "crack is a drug used by poor black people in high-rises shooting at each other, while crack cocaine is used exclusively by rich white types in West London penthouses."

Seb seems to shudder.

"You don't really play the game, do you?" he hisses.

Pete inhales the white fumes, waits a while, exhales and grabs at the nearest audience member, who screams, so he goes over to sit at the piano instead.

"What women don't understand," he slurs after a large brandy, "is that men write love songs to an idea, not a particular woman. They get all upset when you write something that goes 'I love you' and think it's about another woman."

"Anyway, we need to score now, so who's coming with me?" asks Rob.

166

"I would give anything just to be average." Pete says suddenly. "No, I wouldn't actually. But sometimes I have this need to kill myself; I think about it all the time!"

"Have you ever really been suicidal?" Reg calls out.

"I've been really suicidal," murmurs a man in a blue jacket who has been looking through a bookshelf at the side. Pete looks up with a feral stare.

"How suicidal?" he asks, scowling.

"A lot."

"How much then, on a scale of one to ten?"

The man turns to face him, shaking slightly, his voice rising.

"Well what do you want me to say? If I said eight or something you'd just say nine, and ten would mean I'm going to do it RIGHT NOW!"

"Yeah, yeah, you don't look the type," Pete hisses witheringly, scratching his head through his thinning hair.

"I am, I am!" shouts the man, and digs a small curved blade into his wrist and turns it around. Blood licks down his arm.

"Fuck off out of here!" shouts Rob. He has not got them where they are that day by being soft on attempted suicides. Security appear and shove the man out of a side door. Rob takes several of the audience off with him to score.

"You're crap!" shouts Reg. People shush her. Pete lurches over to the toilet on the stage. The walls move at the touch of a switch, allowing the audience to see him in profile, trousers ruckled down.

"Fuck," he says after two minutes, "I'm all jammed up like there's ten of my mates going down the water chute and someone's just put a picture of Maggie Thatcher at the bottom." It has become fashionable, again, to make jokes about the dead leader.

"Is this what women feel when they're in labour? Ah fuck! You see," he continues in a strained voice, "me 'n' Rob, we know we're not banal. We hate that more than death, illness or rejection. We've always been rebels. We knew our bourgeois background wasn't enough. The rest is history."

Reg notices a small plastified sheet of paper tucked in the back of the seat in front. It looks like a menu, but has what she assumes are fire regulations on it.

Pete hides his face in his hands and there is, finally, a loud splash. He lights up a cigarette. As the first molecule drifts out over the audience and hits Reg something echoes inside her. She feels a swelling where her womb should be. She is familiar enough with that. She braces herself for pain, but none comes. Instead she is flooded, from inside and out, with sensations as if she is being tossed gently over and over on firm, soft ropes. Round and round she tumbles. Love! Of course, this feeling has nothing to do with the first flush of identification with the famous creative man – wanting to be like him, wanting to *be* him – which she has admonished her clients about for the last 15 years in her war against low self-esteem. Nothing at all.

Her heart zithers. Barely acknowledging the resolute enmity of the audience around her, Reg pushes unstoppably to the end of the row. As she gets onto the stage, the lights change and the stage turns, revealing the Intensive Care Unit lovingly polished and prepared.

Pete is curled in a ball on the toilet floor, trousers still down. Reg drags him over to the Intensive bed. The irony is not lost on the audience, but since Pete can probably pay for his own medical treatment anyway, it is slightly blunted. These days, you take your satire where you find it; it cannot be guaranteed by entertainers.

Pete is very heavy. His heels drag up the carpet. Reg marvels at his size, the gratuitous scaling-up of him. She puts him on the bed and plugs him into a bank of silent monitors and resting oscilloscopes. She flicks a switch and a soft systolic bedlam of sound fills the auditorium. Pete's head lolls back. Reg rubs his lips with the ointment. Her actions hiss and hum from individual screens on the back of the auditorium seats and various wired-up pieces of furniture on the set.

She takes off his shirt. His chest rises with perfect breaths. He is nowhere near dead from, or even injured by, his lifestyle. He is a mountain trickled on by acid rain. His body hair pools and flows down to his too peaceful groin. Reg strokes the irregular pile of testicle and smells its harsh metallic fust. She undresses as the music of his body ripples. A tiny clip on his penis releases a hit of Viagra. There is another plastified card tucked between the monitors. They really are assiduous about public safety here.

Reg climbs up and lowers herself onto Pete. The sounds rise and rise. The heart is like drums, the breath and blood are the melody, the harmony is the grinding of skin on skin. The audience leans forward. Pete is barely more conscious than a plant. Reg rocks back and forth. She feels a hot tearing where she herself has no organ. She knows he cannot ejaculate. When the music pillars to its height, Reg becomes all things; animal, tree and spirit.

You and me, we can rule the world! Emperor and Empress of the Underground! Reg would never have thought like that before.

Pete shouts something incomprehensible and falls asleep.

There go your sins, your pains, she thinks, and the waves of the words dance on the screen. She turns down the heartbeat speaker, leaving the breathing. She gets off him, and unclips his penis. Pete lies like a dead stag.

Reg, the tableau's caption might say, has finally found herself a better-known creative man to pair with. She can look forward to a life of fighting off other women and ex-wives, giving birth and indulging in ever more Machiavellian machinations to keep him. She will do most of his work, for which she will be patted on the head, then given a brief footnote at the bottom of a chapter in his biography. That is, if she doesn't kill herself first. For a moment it is almost tempting. Already people are beginning to take an interest in her!

"That was unbelievable!" A young woman rushes up and shakes her hand. "You understand addictions, you understand about the state of health in this country. You know everything!"

Reg tries to calm her.

"I've come all the way up here from the country. I'm addicted, too. I've got this vibrator, and when the battery runs down I go insane. I start running around the room yanking drawers out of their holders and ripping open the remote control. You see, I'd love to work with you sometime. I really would!"

Reg is tired, even more so seeing this woman's fresh face and ideals, and gives her email address in a desultory way. Turning away with deep gratitude, the girl vanishes.

One of the Wolf girlfriends, who was there earlier, comes up. She displays the same familiar state of grace that all these women enjoy. She looks Reg up and down. Reg looks at her. She is one of those one woman walking Mount Athoses. Nothing else female manages to be near her for very long.

"That was brill. Really brill. Would you like to work with us again?"

"Well, actually, I do my own stuff as w—"

"Yes, of course you do. You did read the card didn't you?"

Her eyes are slits.

"Yes!" says Reg. She hasn't.

May you wake up tomorrow, look in the mirror and see a child's body with adult bits tacked onto it, thinks Reg. As she is leaving, Pete comes up to her.

"Give me that card a second. Here's my mobile number. Don't take any notice of her. We'll do something together. Definitely. That was great."

He writes his number in big black letters over the inscription on the card and hands it back.

nine

LUCY AND HER FRIENDS are baiting some Heritage Workers from across the road. The workers frighten easily. They hastily shove their clipboards up their sweaters. When they see the girls cross the street towards them, simultaneously screaming abuse and knocking back small white capsules, they retreat into bunch formation and start shuffling faster. The pills are, in fact, aspirins, but the workers are not to know that. They think the pills are some sort of metamphetamine concoction that will give the children the swiftness and ruthlessness of starving eagles.

Lucy gives a signal. The seven girls surround the little group, holding hands, and dance around them in a ring.

The workers pull out their clipboards and go into tortoise formation, shuddering under their flimsy imitation greatcoats. It is no use trying to get money off them as it is well known that they do not carry any. Instead, they have cards which enable them to get free refreshments anywhere during their working day.

"We're the people your children warned you about," whispers Lucy harshly, looking up at a trembling man with a floppy blonde forelock.

"Yeah, we're anarchists!" spits Kerri, viciously.

"No we're not," snaps Lucy, turning on her. "We're not anything, we're us."

Sensing schism, one of the workers relaxes slightly and catches the eye of the man next to him, a black man not entirely at ease with his role in Heritage. Instantly, Lucy pulls out a battery operated electric prod she found in a drawer in her parents' bedroom and applies it to his knee. He leaps and screeches. As one the group flee, bashing past the girls. Kerri wants to chase them but Lucy holds her back. There's no way they're going to start killing people this week. They're not nearly good enough yet.

Reg, asleep in an armchair, dreams a huge lizard is screwing her, its tongue flashing over her face, the scales on its stomach grinding minutely against hers. She turns over. Its body is surprisingly light. It holds itself in a very well-mannered, delicate way, its geometric dewlaps brushing her head. Later in the dream, after they've fucked and the lizard has sucked contemplatively at a blade of grass for a while before shooting off into the undergrowth, she senses a buildup of knots inside her. A cheeky nodule rises and falls under her flesh. It marches up and down her body, her skin pulling to white as it explores. It is quickly joined by others which dance and rub themselves together. Then, as one, they mass. She watches them coming up her body in arrow formation, over her chest, rising to a point to mimic a third breast, then heading up her neck. She thinks she can foil them by spitting them out, but they are too clever, and travel into her brain via her glands.

Reg wakes. She is taken by the sudden urge to scrub the flat, to pick hairs out of the carpet, to make ready for something. She bustles into the lab and begins tutting at the smell of the animals. That's what all the books told her, when she was little –

all those Eastern European fairy tales with princesses shaped like lollipops – that you should prepare yourself for the onset of official love as if for a nuclear attack. She rushes around the flat piling up her possessions. As she shores them up, she realises that she has never noticed they were so randomly placed, so liberated in their positioning. She thinks about Pete again. She has almost forgotten him while preparing for his arrival.

She must be half asleep to have caught herself nesting like this! She goes to look in the mirror. She looks like a different person. Reg pulls her long wiry hair to the front to make herself look more feminine. There is a ring on the bell. She pushes the intercom button. Someone asks if there are any unaffected women in the house.

"No," she growls.

Reg shuts her eyes. Out of the darkness come fantasies. One cuts through the rest. She is at a smart, fashionable party. Suddenly she stands in the middle of the white fluffy rug and begins to shit a great articulated worm, on and on, garlanding the tables and low chairs. The scene changes. She sees a long queue ahead of her, a muted procession walking towards her openings. She is an ark, an ark of life, of frenzied covenants. Reg watches as every living shape and form creeps, leaps, swims, dives, marches, shuffles into her, the tap and pad of feet at her entrance as her bows fill with them.

Lucy comes in.

"I think you should go and find those blokes again before they find me. You can take my prod."

"Lucy. They're dead. You were there. No-one's been back, have they?"

"But maybe there's some other blokes. Why did they want to get me anyway?"

"To get at me, I suppose. Look. I've got a visitor coming later on. Another artist. Do you want to help me tidy up?"

"No. I'm going to watch TV. If you're gonna do something with him and my mum, I don't want to be here."

Reg waits until Lucy's gone before going out. She walks across town to the dead scientists' flat. There is an officer guarding the door, looking bored and knackered. She easily talks her way past him. Once in the building she realises how tired she is, how sick of everything, how sick of sickness. Her mind is cooking too fast. As she pads up the stairs, she begins to believe she will give herself up to whoever is there. She'll give her power to whoever needs it, if they can just cure the sickness so that everyone shuts the fuck up and goes home, stops leaving town, stops crapping about.

The flat is cordoned off with tape. She walks in. The place is a mess. She goes through the bathroom door. There is blood in the bath, not much but enough, perhaps, for the person to have needed stitches. The back room is open too.

Someone has made a half-hearted attempt to take things with them, but a trail of papers and slides remains, leading towards the door. Reg sits down to read.

At first, it's all very familiar stuff. X chromosome inactivation, women, tabby cats, colour-blind boys. Then Reg finds a memo.

While the inactivation of the X chromosome appears to be random, merely bringing the female down to the level of the male, we have been experimenting with the idea that there could be some choice in the matter. A self-administered injection could be developed to prevent a disease, such as Cystic Fibrosis, being carried. A switched on X could merely be switched off before procreation, thus eliminating the disease. To have a working model for this by June would be most desirable. After that, the elimination of inherited tendencies to heart disease or cancer could be examined.

Under this, someone typed:
We could change all women for good! No more fat arses and saggy tits!

Below that, in handwriting:
No more neurotic paranoid 28 day premenstrual bullshit! No more

tendencies to wonder where significant other's got to after 12 o'clock! No more fucking female aggression! Paradise here we come!

Time passes. It gets dark. Reg finds a small lamp.

The Paradise Project, by James Oake and Philip Jackson. The world's first exploration of Selfish DNA, otherwise known as 'junk'. We made an astounding discovery when exploring the function of the majority of human DNA, which at first appeared to be merely DNA past its sell-by date, evolutionary effluvia which scientists hitherto have got nowhere with. Under a microscope, we fertilised an egg, simultaneously injecting it with a random extract of 'junk' DNA taken from a paid guinea pig.

We went out of the lab for a break. When we returned we were surprised to see that there had been considerable activity on the slide. In fact, it had started to emit a dark honey-brown substance which was quite solid and, on first viewing, was about the size of a large marble. As we watched over the next ten minutes, the blob grew to the size of a table-tennis ball before collapsing and dripping down the side of the microscope.

Tests of the substance proved inconsequential until applied to rats, whose behaviour changed dramatically, and carried over into the next generation. Refer to Classified for details of the changes.

There is a collection of newspaper cuttings about female violence and the breakdown of the family.

Time to go. Reg runs down the stairs, just managing a calm walk by the time she gets to the door.

She gets home. Pete is waiting. Lucy has let him in. Reg was gone four hours.

"I've left Neuremberg. For you, Regina. Can I use the phone," he asks, picking it up. He is on the phone for nearly two hours, during which time he drops several names, of people as well as some very high class establishments. He also uses the word 'frontline'. He seems a versatile, flourishing conversationalist.

Reg waits. While she is waiting she mends four pairs of tights, silly to waste them, glues a plate together and paints over the scuffs on the back of the front door. Some of these chores have been waiting to be done for over a year. She uncorks some wine and spills it into two glasses.

"Sorry about that."

"So you want to work with me."

"Well, Regina, I'd say so."

"You see the thing is," Reg is eager, "there's something I've been working on for the last few months. After seeing your show, I thought we should join forces and get something together."

"Well, Regina, tell me more." He moves his hand over her knee.

"You know the Human Genome Project. Well, I reckon it's not all it's cut out to be. I think it's a perfect time to unleash a scientific satire on the public," her voice rises, "a living exhibition of genetic p—"

"Regina, I love your energy. Can you pour me another drink? A large one of course. As you know, I have very special needs." His hand moves up her leg as she pours.

"—genetic poetry! It's the most exciting thing I've ever done!"

"Oh-ho, Miss Worldly-Wise! Have you ever fixed cocaine, heroin and speed all at once, with four Dihydrocodeines and half a bottle of Laphroig, while driving along Oxford Street with one foot on the wheel and a hooker going down on you at the same time? Now that would be the most exciting thing *you've* ever done."

His finger strokes her clitoris. Reg's gusset is a dim-witted collaborator.

"But it's new, timeless, and—"

They press their chests tensely against each other, like birds about to fight. They kiss; their lips are cold, the rest of their bodies colder. Reg feels her body motion beneath its perfumed chrysalis, but it seems to be directed from somewhere else, as if she were radio-controlled. Pete leers a home-strait leer.

Reg pulls out his genitalia and mounts him, the corrugations of his zip cold against her. He is the plinth to her statue. He is barely hard. Pete grips her thighs under her concertina of clothing. She takes her left hand and etches herself to orgasm through the bright acid gleam of her vulva. Pete comes a poor click of come before letting out a snore like a pteranodon's retch. She hadn't, at first, considered the fact that Pete might also be addicted to sleep.

A wave of bitterness comes over Reg as Pete snores. She goes into the lab and kills every creature that is not already dead, picking the smaller ones up by the tail and banging them on the table, smothering the rest. She mixes up as many sleeping pills as she can find and pours them down Pete's throat, then improvises an Intensive Care function for the bed. She'll have him.

Five days pass. Pete is still snoring. The weather is on the turn. The air has relaxed and the trees are getting green. People do not hunch any more as they walk. News reports drearily trot out the latest figures; reporters wait in stations for women to interview. Pete snores.

Reg begins a new phase of the experiment. Her daily structure is as rigid as it was once fluid. Alarm clock, bundle of fresh vegetables from Lucy, turn Pete, wash, start work. Her surroundings become more and more irrelevant as her day dreams become more concrete. Fear of being caught, for her enemies will undoubtedly perform experiments on her, is crowding round her thoughts, making a gangway for hate alone. Reg has never been much of a hater. Hate is so time-consuming. But now it jostles at her.

Johnny is there, in her head. He has been sitting in her thoughts, waving to her through the mass of preoccupations of the last weeks. Reg fixes on his image and speculates. He feels so powerful, so Masonic, that the world seems to spin around him as if he is the sun. Reg will get him. He will look into his pubic hair and see eggs clinging to the dense black shafts. Oh, crabs, he will think, now how did I get those? And he will begin picking the sticky ova from himself. As he watches, they will begin to vibrate and hatch. What comes out of the tiny shells will not be lice but full size Yorkshire Terriers, their flesh trembling under wispy beige hair, their cute forelocks merging with their stringy little beards. They will scamper, jostling for space, between his legs. He will howl.

Lucy and her girls enact plan A. In formation they travel to her old school. Her former classmates are sitting under the spring trees with their milk, lying back as if in paradise, making daisy chains. Lucy and the girls climb the wall and stand on top of it, holding onto the security wire, staring. The chief Steal, temporarily, at least, not chief of anything because Steel Hempen are really out, out, out, looks at them. Her red hair is unmistakable. The girls stand and look. Gradually the playground goes silent. There is only the sound of the trees in the wind and a concrete mixer in the next road. A pale face appears at a window, and out comes a teacher. The same one as before. She advances nervously, shawled, towards the fence. She would like to go home forever. She is now one of two remaining woman teachers in the school. She has been helping train a plumber, two marketing consultants and an ex-drummer to teach maths, English and French. She is very stressed.

"Would you get away from there, please. You're distracting my pupils." Her pupils. She wishes they were all dead. As one, Lucy and the girls hurl themselves at the wire and begin barking, howling and spitting, their bowler hats bobbing.

"Come and get us then," sings Lucy, taking her hat off and shaking it, regally. They jump down and run.

Time passes. Pete snores. Reg drags him into the lab and sets to work.

ten

IT IS ALREADY HOT IN THE EARLY MORNING SUNLIGHT. The day's heat squats over the city, pressing down on it like a shield. In the dark where the sun has not yet reached, the dawn mist is slipping quickly away from the already sweating masses. It is going to be one of those days so hot and shiny-bright that half the people will rush out and embrace it before they know what they are getting into. The other half will stay at home, maddened and flattened by the obligation to enjoy themselves when they cannot. The weather has brought a foreignness into the air, buoying up the nation as it floats on its ready effluent of school songs and commemorative statues. This is a nation suffering from emotional scurvy.

A huge inflatable gas balloon in the shape of the human body hangs above the city, half a kilometre long, pink, shimmering. There are few clouds to compete with it. No-one has considered its position in relation to the sun. Flyer upon flyer has been forced through letterboxes in the past weeks; demonstration and counter-demonstration planned. News reporters are desperate to find stories that have nothing to do with women or children. Giant rats and cockroaches are 'discovered', and there is a lot of coverage of a man who grinds up and eats new stretches of motorway as a protest against road-building.

Across the Atlantic, politicians make speeches of encouragement. Insurance companies are poised to rewrite every policy. Millions have trained as counsellors for those with defective histories. In England, however, fat men in red coats and tricorn hats shout, "Oyez! Oyez!" and ring large bells, while hundreds of low-paid volunteers hand out badges and caps saying, "I won the human race."

Reg can feel her mascara melting although it is only 7 a.m. The criers have woken her, over the roaring of lorries and the belting of generators.

Two months have passed. Reg is pale. She cannot stand being indoors any more. Pete snores in the lab. Reg pushes past the tubes and wires dangling like lianas and pulls up the blind.

She looks out and sees a skein of tattered bunting flapping gently against the hideously bright blue sky. Hot summer days in the city fill her with horror. They force you to go outside, to grab picnics, to get into cars and sit on stinking roads for two hours in order to get somewhere packed with other people doing the same thing. Such a day looked at through glass is even worse, the smoky sheen on the inside forcing the distance even more. Lucy phones her from upstairs.

"Lucy, it's midsummer day. I'm going to let you in, but just you, yeah."

Lucy runs downstairs and waits for Reg to unblock the door.

"There's some locusts outside, but they're all dead. Fuckin' 'ell!" Lucy catches sight of Pete.

"It doesn't smell bad though, you must admit," says Reg.

"Reg, you look fucking awful." Lucy is brown. They have all been sunbathing on the roof. Lucy goes into the lab to stare. The phone rings.

"That Regina?" It's Kerri, sounding frightened. "Regina, Lucy says she's seeing stuff, visions and that. Monsters and people on giant horses 'n' stuff. We was gonna go selling the hats today and take out a few Heritage blokes. But no way, if she's gonna suddenly sit down an start rabbittin' about six hundred foot waves and gigantic red sewing machines with hyper-dermics coming out of them with, wot was it?" There is mumbling in the background, "Yeah, people on a conveyor belt or something."

"What about the locusts?"

"Oh no, they're real. Look outside."

"Why don't you just go yourselves?" says Reg. "I need her with me for a while." There is muffled discussion.

"Is that OK with her?"

"Yeah." Reg laughs.

Four hours later, Reg leaves Lucy in the flat, shows her what she has to do and tells her to sit by the phone. Shaking, Reg goes down the stairs. The movement has become temporarily alien to her, and she lurches slightly.

Reg staggers in the heat. There is a smell of burning onions in the air. There must be a burger van up the road somewhere. Men wander everywhere. The ratio now is about ten men to one woman. The latter walk with a mixture of pride and fear.

Reg walks towards the park. She bristles at every overheard conversation. She thinks she is hearing her name. Her skin tightens under the sun. Figures flicker on the periphery of her vision. A man whistles at her. There are suddenly no other women in sight. He trots after her like an eager bullock.

"You married?"

"Fuck off."

Almost immediately Reg bumps into a fat, suited man who mockingly blocks the pavement. He is huge, and waves his arms to tease her. In one hand he holds a gigantic cigar. Reg flutters to get past. The glowing end almost touches her cheek. The silver surge of agony almost drives her through him, like a great metal bird soaring through clouds.

She walks. There really are a lot of men in the streets. Period costume is everywhere.

"You are pursuing me in my dreams." The voice curdling within Reg is, perhaps, her own, as if she had gone to all the trouble to start a relationship, then found she is obliged to order her partner to dominate her. Her skin tingles. She walks through the increasing crowds, strangely passive for so many people. They look at her as they part. She walks until she reaches Hyde Park. A huge maypole has been erected, a fiver for ten minutes dancing. Ushers, dressed as Morris Men, march through the crowds.

Black shapes like beetles bob among the crowds. Many of the children are wearing bowler hats.

Reg stands in the crowd, trying to reach into the band of moving air above the stagnant miasma of the faces below her. The rough, body odour scent of burger onions is far more like the real thing than the petrified chemical smell that comes from actual bodies. The frothy beer is warmed in the sun and weakened by saliva. The milkshakes, hundreds of them, are scentless, government approved. But none of this is working as well as it should, and there are murmurs, particularly around where Reg stands. Somewhere in a tree above her a group of birds sing. Thank God for high heels. She can see. The ground is baked hard enough for them not to sink in. Her wig is itching.

There is a rumble from somewhere, from other streets, the seeping heat spreading the sound, sometimes loud, sometimes faint. It is the protest floats, the feeble pang-pang of metal kidney bowls. The unhealthy round the corner, pushed, wheeled, their agony roaring out of them like a tidal wave. There is the Waiting Float, with a spiral of people silent in chairs; there is the Intensive Care float, with beds and tubes dangling dangerously over the crowd like a giant wobbling ribcage. Reg stands, every hair in her flesh vibrating, her make-up crumbling in the rush of suffering.

"We want our NHS back!" the woman's voice is thin, tired. The anniversary barely featured in the run-up to this day.

About five hundred yards away a huge fire burns. People are invited to throw things into it from a special platform. Children with marshmallows are discouraged. It is 30 feet tall. It was not supposed to be lit until the evening.

A trio of teenage boys pass by, wearing "Positively *Charged!*" T-shirts. Reg follows to the sound of piped music. A gold-fringed marquee, glinting in the sun, bears the sign, 'Therapy Tent'. Large men take money from the punters who are queuing quietly. It is cool, dark and crowded inside. Reg gives 20 pounds and sits in the centre of the middle row. The roof of the tent is blue and gold, lit like the interior of an orthodox chapel. There is a star-shaped hole in the roof with small mirrors positioned along the edges of it, which move to reflect the sun in a dense white shaft, down onto a small marble font on the stage. It is full of burning, aromatic oil.

"Mind the light!" warn the bouncers, occasionally holding pieces of paper in the beam, which are consumed instantly.

The spotlights are dimmer than usual. The music stops.

Down the ramp comes Johnny. When the spot goes on him there is a ripple of shock in the audience. He looks years older. His arm is stiff and obviously bandaged beneath his jacket. Reg smiles to herself.

"Look at that ray of sunshine!" he croaks. The silence is thick. A Morris dancer's bells tinkle briefly past the tent's entrance.

"That ray is so dangerous when you stand in it, but smell the glorious smell of the aromatic oil, the priceless aromatic oil. That ray is money, so dangerous in the hand of those who do not know how to use it. That ray is love, so dangerous in the hands of those who do not know how to—"

"That ray is a low-fat yoghurt, so dangerous—" Someone shushes Reg.

Johnny tries to draw himself up.

"Like the sun, love and money are there for us all. They are the tools of life! Look at me. They use words like 'confined' to describe me in my wheelchair. But I am full of life, of love!"

"And money too," murmurs Reg over the sighs of assent. Someone pokes her. Johnny begins a long anecdote about a retired circus clown who tried to set up as a bookie. Reg dials Lucy discreetly.

"OK, the fork."

"OK."

Johnny rhapsodises.

"...offered him ten to one on Pickled Pepper, a known finisher, but the man said – argh!" Johnny gags. The audience looks up, concerned.

"Excuse me, excuse me." A girl brings him a glass of water. He is all right after half a minute.

"But the man said, come on, mate, that's outrageous. Now remember Mr Coco'd been in the business for a whole week by then—"

Reg whispers to Lucy again. Johnny retches even more violently. He sits with his head in his hands.

"OK, the chair," whispers Reg.

Johnny recovers and continues to talk in a strained voice. Everyone in the place begins to see a dark red halo around him. Then there is a slight smell. Johnny is obviously agitated. The chair gets redder and glows.

Reg is shifting in her seat. Discreetly, she lifts the binoculars to her eyes. It is worth it just to see the turmoil in Johnny's face as the reality of the situation dawns. To save himself from hideous injury he must get up.

And then he does. But to Reg's horror, the audience thinks this is a miracle. They stand and cheer. The lights go up.

"Feet, the fucking feet!" Reg hisses to Lucy. "When I say!"

Johnny lurches forward. At the moment his head comes under the beam of sunlight Reg hisses, "Now!"

People all around her are transfixed by his terrible screams. He is smoking like a sconce. Back at the flat, Lucy is appalled by the mess she has made of Pete's body and the couch. Flies are starting to come through the windows, big fat ones.

"Lucy. We did it! That was my show! I've done it!"

Johnny's workers try to save him but cannot. When his voice has dropped to a low moan, Reg sees her opportunity and runs down onto the stage.

"It's a conspiracy, don't you see? It's government experiments on women. They spread poisoned medicine round the community and it went wrong. They've messed with our DNA! It's all mutated and gone wrong! They thought they could make us docile, but there's been a huge establishment cock-up! Remember Ecstasy? That was a conspiracy, too!"

Few people listen. Johnny's body flops off the stage and splats to the ground, leaving a trail. People weep. Someone runs out of the entrance with purpose. Seconds later a group of people come in wearing seventeenth century costume, all high-crowned hats and breeches. Reg passed them earlier on, a bunch of Heritage Workers leafleting.

"Witch!" one of them screams.

"Who turned her neighbours' milk," shouts another, "and threw it in the street? And disrupted the schools? Who fucked animals in her sleep? Who held the door open for a family whose child is now possessed, and who painted pictures with her parents' own excreta? And who caused every good woman in this country to go mad and deny her own children?"

"Drive her forth with staves!"

"No, first let's find the place where the Devil got her evil soul!"

They fall on her and pull her to a van. As they go, Reg sees a couple of children trying to pull off their bowler hats, screaming, their heads smoking. They drive her through the crowds, drag her into a building, up cold marble stairs unbaked by the sun, and X-ray her. The molten white bleeds against the blue as they hold up the transparencies.

"The Devil's mark, where is it?"

"She hasn't got a womb! There's a scar where she puked out her soul for Satan to lick up!" someone shrieks. "This is your doing, these women running away. You reprogrammed them in your own disgusting image!" A women points at her, screaming.

"Is it me? Is it me?" Reg thinks of the banal, enforced images of the Jesus Christ of distant books, the lamb-man with the raised hand. They drag her to a bathroom where a jacuzzi is already boiling. Five of them push Regina's head under the water. She feels her wig and make-up lift up and off her.

"She's a witch!"

"My broomstick a man, my cauldron a woman," thinks Reg. Hundreds of years before, the image of Pan the life-god was gradually redrawn as Satan.

"This is not a woman! She tried to resurrect a dead baby for her foul installation experiments!" someone shouts.

"Let's see if we can make her feel something." Someone approaches with a cast-iron pitchfork and pokes it between her forced open thighs. It sits like a gate against her flesh. Her blood froths in the water.

Resurrect! She did no such thing! The baby was an also-ran for a photographer who was beauty contesting infant corpses for part of his 'Family Group' social comment piece. Reg took it off his hands and replaced its bones with jointed metal struts, all connected to an electronic circuit. Making it walk was not a problem – she wanted it to fly. The main image of her childhood was an old poster of some stern Renaissance frivolity. Flying babies with the inner structure of Leonardo, and the outer of Michelangelo. A shimmer came into the photographer's eyes when she hinted to him what she was doing. She did not mention the little rotor-blades she lovingly constructed in her lab. As a child she was always told, with hindsight rather tactlessly, that babies represented good luck. Every time someone got pregnant or gave birth, people said 'Congratulations', except in the case of her own mother, when everyone was horrified. But resurrect, no, no. The life she gave to the dead baby was entirely one of her own concoction, and bore no relation to the one God had given it previously.

Someone is pushing her head under the hot water. It could be quite a good death but for the pitchfork. As she struggles, she remembers she still has the last bit of ointment. She holds her breath and goes still, inching her hand, which they cannot see properly, under the bubbles. She sticks her finger into the ointment and rubs it on her head before someone catches her arm. She waits.

Her head is hit as if with an iron. She rises out of the water. It is like the first time. She is moving faster than they can see. The water steams and evaporates around her and she runs down the stairs. There are burn marks on the marble. She runs through the frozen silent faces to a mobile toilet where she passes the queue and dives for the sink. She is nearly on fire. She puts her head in the water which boils instantly. She fills and refills the sink until she is cooler and calmer.

She looks out of the door. People are starting to speed up slightly. There is Danny, turning towards her. She runs to him, takes him by the arm and pulls him into a cubicle.

"Danny, I've missed you so much!" His eyes widen and widen as she holds him tightly. She is not hot enough to burn him any more. His whole body starts to shiver. His voice is stretched out and deep. She pushes him down onto the toilet seat and sits on his cock. Tantric style, she remains unmoving. Gradually the noise around them returns and everything speeds up again. Danny is shouting, but for help.

"She's here, she's here!" he screams as the mob approaches.

"Burn her!" they shout.

"Sorry Regina."

Lucy turns off the radio and rests, her mind smoothed by the hum of traffic below and a single pigeon cooing in the gutter by the window. She sleeps for a while, and dreams that a marvellous change comes over all the old things in the city. Tables, chairs, lampstands, ceremonial swords, grandfather clocks, all begin to talk, to emanate everything they have ever witnessed all at once in a gentle, multilingual clamour.

The door bulges and four enormous men barge in. Lucy wakes, thinking for a moment that they are child-catchers, armed with National Insurance numbers and indelible ink stamps.

"Where is she?" The first one's overcoat flaps as he peers theatrically into small cupboards. The other one, even more massive, goes into the bedroom.

"Fwoo! Something's died in 'ere!" he shouts through the miasma of Pete's snores.

"Is that 'er in disguise? Bloody cross-dressing trans-lesbo gender-benders!" says the first man, striding over to Pete and shaking him. Pete lets out a terrible fart which lasts nearly four minutes. However, instead of wafting his hand in front of his nose and frowning, the other man is overcome with a look of absolute horror.

"It's the last trump! Like it said in the memo!"

"Shit!" says the other one, quietly. They both turn and run for it, leaving great drifts in the carpet.

Lucy picks up a large kitchen knife and holds the end delicately between thumb and forefinger. She prods at the palm of her hand. The blade goes straight through effortlessly, coming out of the other side with regal slowness. Lucy does not mind the pain. It alleviates the boredom. She walks into the bedroom. The bed is black with flies. Pete must be dead. The smell has the presence, the density, of another human being.

The doorbell rings again. Lucy smashes the unit with a saucepan. It did not matter. She knows Reg will not come back.

Lucy wants to get rid of Pete. She goes back into the lab. He seems to be breathing, but all she can see are insects.

"Right, you!" she shouts and, holding the saucepan aloft, she marches over to the table and brings it down hard on Pete's head. But Pete is not Pete any more. He is merely an unbelievably dense swarm of flies, the sun glittering green on their metallic backs. Lucy tries to open the window but can't. The atmosphere outside seems to be pushing against it. Lucy kicks at the flies, jumping and jumping on the congealed, crusted table. There is a low hum in the air.

The walls of the flat begin to crack, gently, simply, without fanfare or grind. From them issues thick honey-coloured lava that smells rich and tropical. Lucy watches it fall in jelly-spews onto the floor. Outside, the sky is turning lilac. There are more and more voices, whispering, encouraging, admonishing from the walls. Particularly from the cupboard where Reg keeps her sound effects. Lucy walks over to it.

She opens the freezer, sees the remains of her mother and closes it again. Anything with a history, however short, is speaking. Even the flies have words. The windows hiss and cackle. Lucy walks over to them and tries to look out. Far below, the road is full of humans and cars struggling to merge. Everyone is getting mechanised except her. The resinous matter bursts forth like lips. She licks the honey-brown stripes of ointment as they course down the wall in a gentle rollick.

"It's you," the voices seem to say, mockingly. Lucy lies in the hot mauve gloom. The sunlight outside fades gradually, turning to passive, putrid fluorescence. There is a grinding shriek; as one, every human body bursts and the skin flies away, dried instantly in the heat. All that remain are veined metal structures, vibrating in the reflected light, crouched and ready to spring.

Lucy lies in a patch of light under the window. The amber liquid burns slowly over the floor towards her body. It moves onto her like the palms of a huge hand and, having caressed her, plugs her. Little Lucy, the lone fleshly survivor, is preserved, while all around outside run mindless naked jaws and hungry spines.

CODEX

COBRALINGUS
by Jeff Noon

ISBN 1 899598 16 2 • £8.95UK • $14.50USA • $22.95AUS/CAN • Introduction by Michael Bracewell • Illustrated by Daniel Allington

Cobralingus is the exciting and innovative new collection from the author of *Needle in the Groove*, *Vurt* and *Automated Alice*.

Cobralingus applies the techniques of electronic dance music to the production of words, dissolving language. The **Cobralingus** filtering device borrows text and samples it, manipulating words into new forms.

Please note: **Cobralingus** involves no computational algorithms except for the strangely twisted pathways inside Jeff Noon's head.

NEIGHBOURHOOD THREAT: ON TOUR WITH IGGY POP
by Alvin Gibbs

ISBN 1 899598 17 0 • £12.95UK • $19.95USA $29.95AUS/CAN • With 50 b/w photos

After receiving a call from Hanoi Rocks guitarist Andy McCoy, Alvin Gibbs of the UK Subs embarked upon a global tour with Iggy Pop. 230 nights of Iggy's unique brand of performance in just about every major town and city across six continents.

What seemed like any rock musician's dream gig became an odyssey of surreal decadence. **Neighbourhood Threat** features drugs, booze and professional Japanese groupies. Follow Iggy Pop and his band around the globe as they vomit while Johnny Thunders of the New York Dolls has wild sex on the other side of the bathroom, party hard with Guns 'n' Roses, and pretend to ignore David Bowie.

Originally published in 1995, the new Codex edition of **Neighbourhood Threat** includes previously unpublished photos, an updated Iggy Pop discography, and a new 'Outro' (an update on developments since 1995).

CHARLENE'S ANGELS
by Colin Ginks

ISBN 1 899598 15 4 • £7.95UK • $12.95USA • $19.95AUS/CAN

When queer-bashing culminates in murder somebody must take revenge…

Gus thinks everyone's out to get him – the police, the thugs at the end of the road, even Serge, the gorgeous Bosnian nymphomaniac. Will Gus come to terms with the painful side of coming out, and will he and Serge ever get it on? Or will Charlene, self-styled sex-change gangster, draft Serge into her service? **Charlene's Angels** follows Gus and his friends as they tackle the mysteries of life and death, love and loss, murder and revenge.

Set in Liverpool against a backdrop of saunas and nightclubs, **Charlene's Angels** is a romantic gay thriller featuring a cast of speed urchins, transsexuals and emotional refugees.

CRUCIFY ME AGAIN
by Mark Manning

ISBN 1 899598 14 6 • £8.95UK • $14.50USA
$22.95AUS/CAN

For a decade Mark Manning was Zodiac Mindwarp, sex god, love machine from outer space and frontman of heavy metal band The Love Reaction. **Crucify Me Again** documents the spiralling depravity of his years within the moral quagmire of bad sex, worse drugs and truly horrific rock and roll.

Mark Manning has worked extensively with Bill Drummond of The KLF, co-authoring *Bad Wisdom* and the 'Bad Advice' column for *The Idler*.

'Tales of excess and bravado imbued with a self-deprecating wit' – The Guardian

CHARLIEUNCLE NORFOLKTANGO
by Tony White

ISBN 1 899598 13 8 • £7.95UK • $11.95USA
$19.95AUS/CAN

CHARLIEUNCLENORFOLKTANGO is a 'stream-of-sentience' alien abduction cop novel.

CHARLIEUNCLENORFOLKTANGO is the call sign of three English cops driving around in a riot van. In between witnessing and committing various atrocities and acts of work-a-day corruption, and being experimented on by aliens, Lockie thinks aloud about old Blakie and The Sarge, cave blokes and cave birds and *Charlie's Angels*.

Tony White is the author of *Road Rage* and *Satan Satan Satan!* and editor of the *britpulp!* anthology.

'Utterly brutal, darkly hilarious – the most remarkable novel of alien abduction I've ever read' – Front

DIGITAL LEATHERETTE
by Steve Beard

ISBN 1 899598 12 X • £8.95UK • $14.50USA
$22.95AUS/CAN

Digital Leatherette is a surrealist narrative pulled down from invented web-sites by an imaginary intelligent agent. The ultimate London cypherpunk novel features: the Rave at the End of the World; street riots sponsored by fashion designers; a stellar-induced stock market crash; the new drug, Starflower, and barcode tattoos.

Steve Beard is the author of *Logic Bomb* and *Perfumed Head*. He has written for magazines including *i-D* and *The Face*.

'An exuberant, neurologically-specific, neo-Blakeian riff-collage. I enjoyed it enormously' – William Gibson

CONFUSION INCORPORATED:
A COLLECTION OF LIES, HOAXES & HIDDEN TRUTHS
by Stewart Home

ISBN 1 899598 11 1 • £7.95UK • $11.95USA
$19.95AUS/CAN

Confusion Incorporated brings together, for the first time, the journalistic deceptions of arch wind-up merchant Stewart Home. Regardless of whether Home is being crude, rude or devious, he hits his targets with deadly accuracy and side-splitting effect.

Stewart Home is the author of *Cunt, The Assault On Culture* and *Blow Job*.

'Quick, funny – the outrageous pieces leap off the page with manic energy' – Time Out

CRANKED UP REALLY HIGH
by Stewart Home

ISBN 1 899598 01 4 • £5.95UK • $9.50USA
$14.95AUS/CAN

A lot of ink has been spilt on the subject of punk rock in recent years, most of it by arty-farty trendies who want to make the music intellectually respectable. **Cranked Up Really High** is different. It isn't published by a university press and it gives short shrift to the idea that the roots of punk rock can be traced back to 'avant garde' art movements.

'A complex, provocative book which deserves to be read' – Mojo

"I'D RATHER YOU LIED"
SELECTED POEMS 1980-1998
by Billy Childish

ISBN 1 899598 10 3 • £9.95UK • $17.95USA
$24.95AUS/CAN • Illustrated with woodcuts
and drawings by the author

"i'd rather you lied" brings together a life-time's work of one of the most remarkable and unorthodox voices of the late twentieth century. This volume sees Billy Childish take his rightful place as the poet laureate of the underdog. Includes previously unpublished poems.

A legendary figure in underground writing, painting and music, Billy Childish has published more than 30 collections of poetry and two novels, recorded over 80 albums and exhibited his paintings worldwide.

'His poems are raw, unmediated, bruisingly shocking in their candour and utter lack of sentimentality' – Daily Telegraph

NOTEBOOKS OF A NAKED YOUTH
by Billy Childish

ISBN 1 899598 08 1 • £7.95UK • $19.95AUS
Not available in the USA

Highly personal and uncompromising, **Notebooks of a Naked Youth** is narrated by one William Loveday, an acned youth possessed of piercing intelligence, acute self-loathing and great personal charm. Haunted by intense sexual desires, the ghosts of his childhood and a 7000 year old mummified Bog Man, William Loveday leads us on a naked odyssey from the 'Rust Belt' of North Kent to the sleazy sex clubs of Hamburg's Reeperbahn.

'Childish spits out vicious literary disgust in great gobbets of rancour' –The Big Issue

Coming in early 2001:
MY FAULT

ISBN 1 899598 18 9 • £9.95UK • $15.95USA
$26.95AUS/CAN

The new, illustrated edition of Billy Childish's seminal debut novel.

For more information about these and other titles visit our website at:

www.codexbooks.co.uk

To order by mail, send a cheque, postal order or IMO (payable to CODEX, in UK Pounds, drawn on a British bank) to Codex, PO Box 148, Hove, BN3 3DQ, UK. Postage is free in the UK, add £1 per item for Europe, £2 for the rest of the world. Send a stamp (UK) or International Reply Coupon for the new catalogue/sampler.